WE WERE FREE-RANGE

An American Childhood 1950-1962

WE WERE FREE-RANGE

An American Childhood 1950-1962

By

John Erwin

WE WERE FREE- RANGE is published by
LEMONADE PRESS, a division of
PARADOCS VENTURES, Fort Worth, Texas

Share comments and your free-range stories at the author's website: **www.johnerwinbooks.com** Also, find links for ordering additional paperback copies of WE WERE FREE-RANGE and eBook editions.

Disclaimer: This manuscript is a reflection on the changing nature of childhood. Stories are told from a child's eye view: incomplete, skewed by time, and subjective. Names have been changed and some characters are composites. Superficial detail has been scrambled for privacy's sake. The author hopes his enduring affection for the people and time portrayed is obvious.

ISBN – 13: 978-0615456065
ISBN – 10: 0615456065

DEDICATION

Considering everything my wife, Sue, has endured raising me, a book dedication is pretty sorry compensation. Her years of love and encouragement can't be repaid, but I remember to say "I love you" everyday.

CONTENTS

FOREWORD

Good Eggs

I love my four granddaughters like a fat guy loves cake. Recently, however, there have been unsettling changes in our relationship. The 2-year-old still believes I'm a god while the high-schooler has limited time for any adult. (Nothing personal.) I think the middle girls are spending way too much time with my wife because their comments increasingly are peppered with innuendo I'm not completely competent; that there's probably a better way than mine. (Nothing personal.) The 11-year-old is definitely Grandma's minion.

Now she supervises me in public when my wife is unavailable. A recent grocery-buying trip is a perfect example. My precious granddaughter - the child I taught to stand on one leg - badgered me in Target about eggs!

"Pop-Pop. Are those the ones Grandma gets?

"What do you mean? They're eggs and they're cheap.

"I mean Good Eggs."

"Oh yeah! What are those good ones called? Home-schooled? Self-actualized? Carbon-free? New-World-Ordered?"

"Pop-Pop," she scolded, "You know the only good eggs are Free-Range!"

I smiled and traded out the bargain eggs for Grandma ones. I was teasing, of course. I knew my wife's egg preferences and even why she favored free-range over *pastured, cage-free, organic,* and the like. Essentially, any biotic-free chicken (even one raised for commercial purposes) that forages a natural landscape has the best chance of being the chicken God intended. Pumping growth hormones into a caged chicken will increase size while standardizing meat and egg production, but the resulting creature is a pale version of its natural ideal.

That silly exchange got me thinking about how different her childhood is from those of my wife and me. Our parents never organized play dates; we roamed the neighborhood unsupervised from dawn to dusk and rode in cars without seat belts or power windows. We survived roller-skating and bike rides without helmets or pads. The family shared one bathroom, one television, one phone. And we devoured white sugar by the pound. In short, we were Free-Range. My granddaughter, I fear, is cage-fed.

Lately, I've been obsessing about childhood. I can't explain why these memories have resurfaced lately with such insistence. My wife says preoccupation with the past is proof I've entered the Get Off My Lawn stage. I argue reflection is a necessary first step to wisdom, but mostly it's the fault of my young granddaughters. They make me tell these stories. For them, a 1950s childhood conjures a world as exotic as Harry Potter's or the back of C. S. Lewis' closet.

As special as we feel, everybody carries memories of inordinate weight; storehouses mined most vigorously when we need comfort or assign blame. I wrote versions of some of these vignettes twenty years ago. I recorded them in a paranoid fit when I feared losing my three-year-old son through divorce. Convinced he'd move to another state and never know me, the stories were part of a letter to him I never had to send. Mercifully, life gives more than it takes.

These are stories of childhood, 1950-1962. This is what life looked like before hormones and girls, before Beatles and Vietnam, long before computers and cell phones, and a lifetime before anyone was dismissively tagged *just another boomer*. Relax and return with me now to those thrilling days of yesterday, when all of us were Free-Range Kids.

CHAPTER 1

After the War

You Are Here

Any map I drew of my 1950s neighborhood would resemble those pre-Columbus depictions of Europe and the rest of the planet. The area immediately surrounding *you are here* would be rendered in exhaustive detail, but beyond those few square blocks of home, the landscape would be mist and sea monsters.

Concepts like longitude, latitude, and magnetic north are worthless to me. Compass points not only confuse; they defy reason. I never mastered enough quantum mechanics or string theory to navigate America's highways like other people. I mean, unless Schrodinger's cat is driving, there should be no way an automobile can travel west on I35 North and connect with TX121 South by taking an east exit.

Growing up directionally impaired, I learned to drive using landmarks like Wards, A&W, or a novel billboard. Today, however, that approach is problematic because unique landmarks are nonexistent in my Metroplex. Every stretch of urban freeway repeats the same sequence of 15 national chains every 5 miles in infinitude.

Consequently, when I get lost or trapped on those roadway cloverleaves, I abandon logic. *Quit reading signs,* I remind myself. *Don't think; just feel it.* Then, summoning my best Zen-like intensity, I focus on the distant cluster of tall buildings (where I live) and drive as the eagle flies. *Give me a ship and a star to steer her by and I'll be home shortly.*

Maps are commonly oriented with north at the top. Similarly, wherever I stand, north is always directly in front of me, south behind me, west to my left, and east to my right. I offer these confessions as partial excuse for the inexactness of my neighborhood geography. I guarantee the places I describe once existed, but maybe not exactly where I've placed them. My sense of the world has always been like looking through the wrong end of a telescope. No matter which direction I turn, the past is always in front of me.

My House

My first address was 765 Alder Avenue and my phone number GA(rfield) 4 – 8923. I'm certain of that. No free-range kindergartener left the house without first memorizing that information so it's trapped in my brain's primal layers. As such, ancient factoids are easier to retrieve than a current work associate's last name or the model car I drive. In fact, the only time I'm marginally more cognizant than a fifth grader is when the category is pre-1968.

Like every house on the block, ours had the architectural grace of a shoebox with a gravel roof. A rectangular picture window (the living room) and operable corner windows (bedrooms) defined the stark stucco exterior. Deep flowerbeds of hydrangeas, callas, fuchsias, ferns, and blanketing baby tears ran the length of the house, softening the house's harsh blandness.

Our covered front porch was enclosed slab to fascia board with stretched lengths of chicken wire. Every year the wire trellises held thick clematis vines with cascading passionflowers. After the purple blooms died, swarms of spiky caterpillars stripped the leaves and spun themselves into brown chrysalises. Weeks later, those naked vines trembled from the collective awakening of a hundred new butterflies drying untested wings in sunlight. Together, they were an undulating black and orange wall; each insect driven by singular instinct, oblivious to the greater spectacle.

Our driveway led to a single car garage that wasn't

needed after Dad built a freestanding shop out back. He never replaced the exterior garage door but reconfigured the inside as his business office and Mom's laundry room. My father wasn't the only one to remodel his garage. Without harsh seasonal weather, autos didn't need to be stored indoors and few families had two vehicles so driveway parking was sufficient. Besides, growing families made remodels and additions commonplace. Our tract of houses with nearly identical exteriors and floor plans eventually looked like a collection of custom homes. Although my neighborhood was no country club estate, there was optimism in the omnipresent sounds of amateur builders and the smell of fresh paint.

Waffles, Art, And Ben Franklin

I don't know when parents become more than animated furniture to their children. As a normal, self-involved child, I was concerned about their problems only in terms of how they affected me. I grew adept at gauging when to ask for money or stay up late. I learned waking Saturday morning to Mom slam-banging every pot and pan in the house was not a good omen. Loud cooking rarely is, especially when it produces only bowls of dry cereal. I learned when Dad spent another evening changing the Chevy's plugs and points in the dark driveway (the second night that week), more than responsible automobile maintenance was at play.

Generally, when they fought, Mom sulked and Dad left. My parents were difficult people to live with because the most terrible things weren't said aloud. When they fought, they wanted us to believe it was about burnt waffles. I'd never suggest they should have spilled their guts at some family intervention around the kitchen table. I only wish adults realized they aren't as clever as they think. Children also can conceal their fears.

One accusation that repeatedly surfaced, and the only one my father fiercely denied all his life, was that he was no businessman. Despite his protest, he wasn't a businessman in the conventional sense. He stayed with a task until it was done properly. Sometimes he absorbed the cost of changes on a contracted job rather than argue with clients. He had to be browbeaten before he'd lay off the crew when work slowed, saying he knew they also had families. Maybe it was perfectionism and soft-heartedness or maybe he understood the real cost of some fights. Whatever drove my father's choices, Mom was accurate when she reminded him, "Your men make more money than you."

Traits that endeared Dad to others often made life hell for her. Both my mother and father were occupied by dreams, but Mom dreamed like Ben Franklin. Logical, universal laws structured her universe. To live, one needed an orderly plan. Conversely, Dad championed inspiration and improvisation. "Things will take care of themselves," he promised. That meant somebody else would have to mend the ragged edges and Mom was that somebody.

It wasn't that Dad was incapable of earning good money. More than once we were saved by huge infusions of cash he earned for completing a house. Rather, it was the feast or famine nature of carpenters' work that made her conservative nature seem ever more rigid and shrewish.

If manipulation of wood and metal were as revered as manipulation of numbers or musical notes, society would have pampered my father as they did Einstein, Mozart, and other genius children. Whatever he could perceive, he could build. If my father had been God, the universe would work much better. However, in fairness to Him, Creation would have taken at least sixty days and there would have been serious cost overruns. My mother's genius was providing calm during the storm. She performed her task efficiently and resourcefully for twenty years but not without great cost to her and, I believe, to him.

My mother eventually forgot her worth and suppressed her creativity. My father grew old in a world that settled for faux marble and fotofinish wood. But all that happened many years later. When I was a child, I never doubted their love for me. Their imperfect support and affection was as welcome and steady as gravity. Together they gave us a home and I know they loved each other then. I once saw them kissing in the kitchen.

CHAPTER 2

Atomic Family

Light And Strange Children

I remember the ducks. Their green and white silhouettes floated in a linoleum circle six feet across, contrasting with the industrial beige squares covering the rest of my kindergarten floor. I loved those ducks in the tiles - the only stillness in a room swirling with light and strange children.

The room was chaos constrained by staples and straight pins. Bulletin boards corralled our drawings but still the walls vibrated with primary colors. Near the front of the room were cubbyholes for lunch boxes and sweaters. In one corner was a wooden kitchen, complete with miniature appliances and a dining table. There little boys ate invisible toast and eggs prepared by girls, practicing to become dads and moms. Opposite the kitchen were long tables with padded benches for serious work like coloring or cut and paste. There were only three painting easels in the room so we took turns.

A sliding glass door at the rear of the classroom led to a fenced playground with many rules and warnings. Our yard had a teeter-totter and two-seater swings. A jungle gym rooted deep in sand served as a crows' nest for spying on big kids outside our fence. Compared to our playground, theirs was an immense asphalt sea, stencilled with bus yellow paint for hopscotch and foursquare. Farther was a forest of tetherball poles, a football field, and baseball diamonds near their own pod of classrooms.

We hoped our recesses would coincide with the big kids' but that rarely happened. Usually we were confined to our tiny pond, reduced to swarming the gym, playing king of the mountain and chanting, "Nickel, nickel. Who's got the pickle?" I still don't know what those words mean or even from where we learned them but, when screamed from atop a tubular steel mountain, it was poetry. We had recess often. Perhaps our teacher thought we'd sit still for colors and numbers if she first wore us out. No matter her plan, we had metabolisms of locusts and our tribal frenzy often swept back into the classroom.

I remember the afternoon we made a pact to ignore the bell and continue our play. Teacher yelled from the sliding glass door, "Inside now! To the circle." Since we loved her and had no preparations for protracted badness anyway, we surrendered our bodies. Wordlessly, we fell into boy-girl-boy single file as she guided us with a barrage of *tsks* and light touches. But we weren't tamed. Although I'm certain we looked docile, she couldn't have known that our hearts fluttered like hummingbirds.

Trudging toward the ducks, we did our best imitations of repentance. During recess, the linoleum ducks had been labeled using masking tape and grease pencil. All found their name and sat in cross-legged silence, but even as we obliged -- before the door was shut completely -- a last breeze spun the classroom's planet mobiles and tore drawings from the walls. Standing at the circle's center, our teacher began again, "Now children," and we nodded in unison. Although our collective breathing had slowed, inside we were still frantic like fawns. We were not afraid, but still our bodies twitched with life and the wonder of our flesh. We were learning.

Blue Callas

Considering how vehemently I once fought plates of Brussels sprouts, it seems inconceivable that I should relish them today. Sometimes, age and experience stunts or even reverses prejudice. Other times, an understanding rooted in childhood just grows more unshakably potent each passing year.

I remember using snapdragon blossoms to perform solitary ventriloquist shows when I was very young. I also remember grazing among the honeysuckle vines with neighbour kids. That nectar droplet on the end of a honeysuckle stamen pulled from its flower is still the sweetest taste I know. As pleasant as those associations are, they don't adequately explain the peace I feel when living among flowers. There are no fond childhood remembrances of time spent working the gardens and I'm not particularly talented at raising plants now. Still, since I left home, I have purposely surrounded myself with flowering plants wherever I've lived.

Mom's garden had callas in the spring. Among the carpet of baby tears and a stand of ferns, white lilies towered on thick, single stocks. The calla lily is actually a large white leaf surrounding a yellow flower spike; the leaf is rolled like a square of paper into an open cone. What appears to be the bloom is fleshy leaf and waxen to the touch.

One Easter, my mother cut callas for floral arrangements. While the stocks soaked in a clear vase on the dining table, she gathered wax paper, a wooden rolling pin, and several pieces of colored chalk. First Mom had me tear lengths of wax paper from the roll, which we wrapped around single sticks of chalk. Then, using the rolling pin, we crushed each chalk into fine pastel powder. I was timid at first, remembering lectures about using my own crayons and chalk responsibly. However, with permission to be destructive, I finished quickly.

Then we unfolded all the opaque squares to reveal vibrant piles of pink, blue, green, and yellow dust. Plucking a calla from the water vase, Mom dabbed at the pink chalk and gently rubbed color into the white lily with her fingers. She taught me to do the same and together we finished where God left off. Within minutes, a rainbow bouquet replaced dull white. Blue callas were our favorites,

Years later, I learned most people associate the lily with death. And I have seen white callas at funerals and wept. I have known sorrow that knotted my whole body. I have sat in pews fighting back sobs by bowing my head and studying my clasped, white-knuckled hands. Most often sadness lingered but other times, though a blur of tears, I've summoned my child hands; the ones stained blue, gently stroking color into a white calla leaf.

The Skull And The Snake

It was open house and our turn to visit the teacher. We stood as a family facing her. Mom kept her white-gloved hands on my shoulders, pinching me with increasing severity whenever I fidgeted. She pulled me against her petticoats as she spoke for our family.

Mom was beautiful and animated. Her dress was aquamarine and properly pressed. Her wavy hair was dark and her lipstick bright. My father had positioned himself slightly apart from us. In these situations, he had a way of standing that made him nearly invisible in crowded places. He stood feet together and bent his body slightly forward with his hands clasped, prayer-like, at belt level. He'd cock his head toward his inquisitor and listen with his intent eyes but rarely offer more than agreeing nods.

This night, Dad wore a green, plaid coat and wide somber tie. His loose-fitting slacks were brown. His thinning hair was Brylcreemed straight back and wire glasses sat atop his hawkish nose. As Mom and the teacher spoke, he slipped away to the other side of the room. Still in Mom's grip, I watched him lean closer to inspect a wall of crayon tracings. Finally, he mouthed the words, "That's my boy." In my head, I could hear how he'd say that, resonant and soft.

A brief smile stretched across his face, which exposed some crooked teeth. I never saw him laugh wide-mouthed, doubled over until years later when he bought an upper plate. I don't remember him unhappy but he usually smiled with pursed lips to contain a straggly front tooth. I never thought of him as self-conscious about his teeth. I certainly wasn't ashamed of the way he looked. Instead, my father was my earliest source of awe. After all, he had a black tattoo on his left forearm of a skull with a snake crawling out one of the empty sockets.

I remembered being cradled in his lap while we watched TV from the living room couch. I'd pretend to fall asleep. I'd dig my head into his side and nuzzle his thick shirt, my hand pushing aside the dark hair and tracing the tattoo with my small fingers. Maybe to hide it, he wore long sleeved shirts even during summer. He never wanted to talk about where or when he got it. That information fell among vague, infrequent references to being young and doing poorly in high school, racing old cars on twisting roads, and joining the Navy during The War. He rarely spoke about who he used to be.

My father was a small man but trim and strong. Suits and ties swallowed him up. He belonged in his wheat-colored carpenter overalls and flannel shirts and heavy laced boots. That always will be the way I think of him.

CHAPTER 3

Sibling Rivalry

Fun With Phonics

We were transporting our grade school granddaughters for a weekend stay at our apartment. From the backseat, the older entertained us with her academic prowess, as she is prone to do. "Grandma, I know all my continents. Wanna hear?"

"Ooo! I know my continents, too," her sister interrupted.

"No you don't. Listen Grandma..."

"Do too!" the younger insisted.

"Listen. North America, South America, Europe, Africa, Asia, Antarctica....Antarctica...Antarctica..."

Realizing her sister had blanked, the little one took smug pleasure from completing the sequence. "And sometimes *y*," she said proudly.

The younger granddaughter often reminds me of Sister Diana, at least the way Diana used to be. There's no biological basis for similarities; it's just temperament and an outlook they share. Both were verbal very early, perhaps from competing in environments where everyone else was older. However, regardless of intelligence, developmental lags are commonplace. Sometimes those lags manifest themselves in misheard phrases and strange leaps of logic.

Diana's earliest speech provided endless amusement. As a toddler, she used to peer out windows and lament *the frog* was rolling in and how sad she felt when it was *froggy* outside. Among her favorite kid foods were *smashed potatoes* and *corn on the cop*. She loved dance troupes on Ed Sullivan but her favorites were *flamingo* dancers. At 8 years old, Diana once returned empty-handed from a shopping errand because Piggly Wiggly sold butter three for a dollar but Mom only wanted one. When she was 10, Diana declared she'd never work at the corner convenience store. Since it was open 24 hours a day, she reasoned she'd have very little time off. For the fifteen years I lived with her, my sister never took a shower without yelling through the locked bathroom door, "Does the shower curtain go in or out?"

Before my baby sister was old enough to play outside alone, she spent an inordinate amount of time staring through screen doors or with her hands pressed to windows. When old women joked they'd like to take our infant brother home,

Diana packed him a suitcase. For whatever reasons, nature or nurture, Diana preferred the circle's outer edge.

My young granddaughter seems to need that distance, too. During family gatherings, she is as likely to observe as demand our attention. I've grown accustomed to her retreats for silence or losing herself in books and movies. As her grandfather, I fret how difficult it must be sometimes. She can do nothing her sibling hasn't already done and done well. Accomplishments that earned applause for the oldest buy her half-hearted notice at best. If I were second-born, who would I be?

Babe

Considering the re-election of Eisenhower and his sidekick, Dick Nixon, was the year's biggest story, 1956 is not particularly vivid in the memories of older Americans. It was, however, significant for my family because of my brother's birth. Our parents named him Frank Lee, but my sister and I called him Babe.

Babe was the youngest of three children born three years apart. Judging from our collected baby books, however, we weren't raised by the same parents. As the first child, my books' coverage begins a few hours after conception and takes six volumes before I'm pictured eating solid food. This handsome, bound set includes an appendix of exhibits like shower announcements, hospital name bracelet, locks of hair, etc. Sister Diana's photo collection is significantly smaller, but being a girl preserved the novelty of picture taking. In contrast, one of two photo albums purchased for Frank's keepsakes is still in its original tissue-lined box. The other book contains only a B&W of Babe's second day home, a Sears "Christmas with Santa" photo taken when he was nine, and a newspaper clipping announcing his high school commencement. It would be wrong to conclude each succeeding child was loved less.

Children's growth is celebrated but adults also grow, becoming more adept and graceful in their roles. In some sense, children of the same family are raised by different parents. The first child is trauma and constant vigilance. A second child is an opportunity to correct mistakes made with the first. However, by the time a third baby enters the home, once complex and contradictory theories about child-rearing have been reduced to *don't sweat the small stuff.* Frank definitely was loved, but he was born into an already highly structured household. Babe never fought for position, he simply fell into line. Not only was he raised by adults, but by siblings as well.

To his credit, Babe never grew artful enough to hide his emotions. Everything important about him can be read in his face. Frank was scrawny as a child, although he had a little potbelly even as a toddler. Most noticeable in early photos are his toothy grin and feisty-old- man-hands-on-hips stance, the face tilted upward like a dutiful flower following the sun. Sometimes the eyes in those ancient photographs also betray a good-natured confusion. They look too old for a child. He appears to be someone who badly wants to believe the world is good but lacks proof.

Although not lonely, Babe was preoccupied and innocently strange. As toddlers do, he spent hours in conversation with inanimate objects. That's not particularly uncommon except he never entirely outgrew that stage. Lost in a parallel world, Frank was oblivious to our laughter at his antics. "Come on, men!" he'd yell over his shoulder at invisible troops. "Follow me!" Then, alone, he'd zigzag across the yard while providing commentary in six different voices and artillery sound effects as needed.

When he was five or six, a common sight from our kitchen window was Frank running atop the six-foot high wooden fence only to take a bullet to the heart and fall dead into Mom's chrysanthemums. Of course, his body had to convulse a few minutes and his little feet make three spastic kicks in the air before he could die properly. (At that point, all any of us knew about death came from Tom and Jerry cartoons.)

For most, innocence is a temporary state; its loss the payment life extracts for adult pleasures. Babe was the kind of kid who cheered ants that hoisted crumbs. He felt the wood's hurt when other children carved trees. He cried over cartoons. We allow children such indiscriminate depth of feeling, but scorn the adult who crosses boundaries of appropriate sentimentality. In many ways my brother is still an innocent and that is what I love best about him. Paradoxically, his life has been more difficult than mine because his heart has always been better.

Divide And Conquer

As the youngest, being an easy target was Frank's birthright. As the oldest, both Frank and Diana clamored for my attention so naturally I amused myself by pitting them against one another. Not that they needed prompting. Early sibling alliances were liquid and changed daily, sometimes hourly. Frank and I were most consistently close during our sister's boys-are-stupid-so-stay-out-of-my-room stage, whereas Frank became the outsider when I entered my teens. The three-year gap between Diana and me mattered less during early high school. Because her accelerated interest in boys coincided with my clueless ways with girls, briefly we were bonded by not only blood but mutual hormonal bewilderment called *adolescence.* ("I'll tell Margie you like her if you'll tell Tom I think he's cute.") From the start, Brother Babe was the designated victim.

Regarding Frank, our parents never gave instructions more

specific than, "Protect your little brother. He trusts you." I'm sure they meant to instill some code of familial allegiance, but such statements only triggered schemes of gentle cruelties. One prank that never went beyond planning was teaching Babe the wrong names for things. We thought it would be hilarious to point to the refrigerator and say *couch*, point to the cat and say *tree*, or point to Dad and say *poop*. It was a potentially wicked concept but years beyond our fledgling abilities.

A more typical, long-running gag involved Diana or me faking our own death in front of Frank. Between us, we decided who was to die. The other's task was to confirm the death, inform Frank it was his fault, and then outline an act of repentance that would both absolve guilt and resurrect the dead. For instance, to keep from losing a board game, I only had to grab my throat, make exaggerated gurgling sounds, and fall to the floor. Frank's eyes went big and teary as he cradled my lifeless face. Then Diana deadpanned, "Well, that's really great, Frank. You just killed John." She'd pause for effect before adding, "But I think cereal would save him."

At that point, I'd stir slightly and mumble, "Yes…(cough)…Trix…(cough. cough)…I need Trix" and off Frank ran for the healing Trix. Of course, cereal immediately replenished my strength and Frank clapped and laughed from relief. Amazingly, this ploy worked many times, although even Frank eventually grew suspicious. During one particularly rough sell, Mom inadvertently became an ally.

I was lying on the floor again and Frank was arguing with Diana when Mom entered carrying an armful of dirty laundry. "John's not dead, is he, Mom?" Our mother, without missing a beat, looked at my prone body and nodded twice.

"Oh, he's dead alright," Mom said as she stepped over my corpse on her way to the washer. Predictably, Frank went into hysterics but that day Diana and I decided our mother was cool. Anyone who believes children are innately kind either never lived with siblings or has a very selective memory.

Clean Plate Club

With a brother as trusting as Babe, gall was our only restraint. Our home practiced the then fashionable you-don't-leave-the-table-until-your-plate-is-clean style of family dining. I'm not convinced my folks really cared about starving Chinese children, rather I think guilt was a strategy learned from their folks. Mom and Dad were not opposed to spanking, but they weren't indiscriminate paddlers either. Their preferred method of discipline was to point out the problem and wait for us to make the *right* decision. Consequently, Diana, Frank and I spent an inordinate portion of our childhoods sitting silently at the dinner table, staring sullenly at heaps of cold mashed potatoes and green vegetables. On those nights, as Mom cleaned the kitchen and Dad read his newspaper in living room, our whispered negotiations began.

"I'll drink your milk if you'll eat these peas."

"Oh sure. You take my liver. I'll drink my milk and trade for that corn."

"You're stupid. Corn's okay. Try eating these potatoes....making me choke."

"Yeck. Gonna throw up."

It always came down to that. Cold mashed potatoes. Eventually, our combined adult experiences included Vietnam, childbirth, and extended hospitalization, but even today the mention of cold mashed potatoes triggers an involuntary gag reflex in all three of us. As kids during prideful battles of will, there were few winning options. One possibility was to wait out Mom and Dad. Eventually they had to send us to bed, but we also lost a night of TV.

If Mom's resolve weakened, we could fake illness and negotiate a few bites of everything on the plate. This solution had the duel advantages of being relatively painless for us and giving her a symbolic victory. A third strategy, cruel but preferred by Diana and me, was distract Frank and shift uneaten goop to his plate. "John and I have cleaned our plates, Mother. May we please have dessert?" It was shameful how we enjoyed our creamy chocolate pudding while Babe, whose plate was covered by a stone cold mountain of potatoes six inches high, sat between us and quietly sobbed face down on the table.

CHAPTER 4

Wait 30 Minutes . . .

Home On The Range

Our house was sandwiched between Alder Avenue and Encina, a.k.a. Suicide Hill. To reach school, I walked Alder, passing the Martins, a vacant lot used for baseball, and Ronny Reynolds' corner house on Alder and 7th Street. The sidewalk ended there but elementary school was just around the corner. Coincidentally, my best friends lived on the same side of Alder, except Thomas whose house was across from Ronny's. Thomas was a loner but nice. He was famous for befriending the garbage men who let Thomas ride on the back of their truck every Monday.

Unless we had permission to walk to the beach, our world stretched pretty much from 7th to Palm Avenue (where there were stores and a movie theater) and back to Alder by way of

9th. Our east property line was a drainage ditch overgrown with pickle weed. The Gully ran under the road and all the way to store trash bins that we trawled for boxes. Back on Alder, across The Gully, lived the McCarthys. They were the neighborhood's Catholic family with 10 kids and a Corvair.

Behind our house row was Suicide Hill whose incline was so steep no child had ever ridden a scooter down it without sustaining life-threatening injury. At the base of Suicide Hill lived the Pomegranate Lady who stole my cat; her house built in the center of a grove and made entirely from French glass doors with crystal knobs. Encina also accessed The Field, a secret wilderness known only to us.

Lost World

In Southern California after The War, houses couldn't be built fast enough. The Field resulted from a sloppy collision of three housing developments. Somehow, in the contractors' haste, no one claimed the irregularly shaped buffer amid acres of competing tract homes and it remained vacant for years. Smack in the middle of civilization was Mr. Edgar Rice Burrough's Land That Time Forgot. It was the wildest piece of nature we city kids knew.

Our field didn't have big shrubs or trees, just dabs of scrubby undergrowth where creatures lived. Most of the land was covered by wheat grass that moved like ocean swells when the wind blew. Foreign birds carried there by sea storms nested in the brush, velvet ants tried to crawl up your legs, and dragonflies clogged the air. Dare to turn over a rock and something creepy scampered out.

Like Marco Polo, we hunted field creatures for the amazement of people back home. With armored body and stegosaurus head, horny toads were always prizes. Their flat bodies were rarely bigger than silver dollars and had smooth yellow underbellies speckled with black. Sometimes we caught one sunning on rocks, but just as often, they hid in hot sand with only their spiky heads protruding. Horny toads look evil but their only defense is to puff up like blowfish. Jerry claimed their eyes bleed big drops when really scared, but I never witnessed that myself.

Like all smart people, I avoided field snakes but alligator lizards didn't faze me. Scary or not, their speed and detachable tales make lizards harder to catch than horny toads. Grab one by the tail, most likely he'll escape and you'll be left holding still-wiggling lizard flesh. On top of everything else, lizards bite so it's best to clamp the mouth shut between thumb and forefinger.

I've heard lizards re-grow missing tails but I can't personally verify that either. If true, it would make sense of Tim's encounter with a fork-tail. The creature he found had a shorter tail attached an inch below the tip of its regular tail, like a small branch on a tree's main trunk. Tim pinned the lizard's head against the dirt and tried to steady its thrashing body. That's when the branch tail popped off. Tim was so surprised he lost control and the creature disappeared. As proof, Tim kept the tail in a matchbox for weeks until his mom threw it out. Nobody believed Tim, but I'm telling you it happened.

The Pond

Our pond was reborn yearly when spring rains came. Whoever discovered the first strands of frog eggs spread the news like a scout bee to the hive. From that day forward, the pond's muddy banks swarmed with muddy kids making the annual pollywog pilgrimage.

Really impatient kids gathered the frogs' gelatinous egg strips, which resembled the red, perforated rolls of caps used in our six shooters. Since pond eggs didn't always hatch, I waited for tadpoles. Besides, I needed extra time to find a suitable jar and soften up Mom. In my experience, the best pollywog farm is a gallon-size glass pickle jar. Although water sloshes through a lid punched with breathing holes, any cover reassures mothers that pollywogs won't be leaping about their house at will.

The easiest way to catch pollywogs is to place an open jar

on its side; half submerged in The Pond's shallows. Eventually, without coaxing, they swim inside. Since nobody knew what tadpoles ate, it was common practice to add a scoop of mud or nearby grass in hope proper food was contained in the surroundings.

I learned not to underestimate the importance of preparing Mom for pollywog season. Without preapproval, my jar wound up in the garage. Since stagnant water gets pretty stinky, it was easier to argue the educational value of a household tadpole farm before stench was an issue. I had a great spot for a farm atop my dresser against a window. New jars stayed cloudy for a couple days, but light from my window illuminated the pollywogs wriggling through suspended silt. Backlighting made the jar a TV screen with bad reception. Sometimes in the murky water I saw black zeppelins battling in the clouds. Other times they looked like whales plumbing the ocean's depths.

By the time my tadpoles grew hind legs and their tails shrank, the jar's contents had settled into a pretty amazing underwater scene, with pieces of reed and clumps of grass anchored in the bottom mud. The tadpoles didn't resemble guppies anymore but they weren't quite frogs either. Actually, even with four legs, they weren't frogs; they were toads that just needed water at birth. After growing legs, instinct drove them toward land. Mom pretty much tolerated one frog, one snake, one lizard, and so forth. It was when creatures traveled in multitudes of biblical proportion that she became unreasonable.

Consequently, Mom insisted all teenaged pollywogs return to The Pond before they matured. But that didn't stop them from visiting us later. Some seasons, there were so many that Dad made piles of toads using a bamboo rake. Whenever that happened, Mom refused to let us outdoors until the croaking army passed through. You would have thought the ground was poisoned with radioactive fallout. From my window, it was impossible not to speculate which toads had slept in my room when they were younger.

The Raft

Since our pond was a product of weather's vagaries, it existed only a few months each year. In addition to toads, the unusual conditions also produced alien insects and exotic vegetation with similarly limited life spans. One plant had air-filled pods that popped like bubble wrap when squeezed. Another's thick, green stocks turned rust with time. Grabbing the dried stocks left seed in your hand that looked like uncooked oatmeal but was only good for making more weeds. Even after the water dried up, the spongy ground supported a stand of bamboo until the steady rains returned. The stalks spread like Triffids.

When full, our pond covered enough ground that someone always contemplated sailing across it. Unfortunately, none of us had sailed a raft much less built one. Our only voyages had been imagined in chapter books. My dad owned carpenter tools, but I was afraid to ask because he'd either think rafting was a dumb idea or be too enthusiastic. Once I wanted help rounding the edges of a stick that held my kite string. I figured smooth edges would allow the stick to turn easier in my hands while letting my kite out or reeling it in. By the time Dad finished helping, my stick was replaced by two-feet of handle from Mom's garden shovel.

Attached to the handle section was my seawater fishing reel and four metal screw eyes to guide the string. The contraption was like a compact rod and reel but for flying kites instead of catching fish. I never said it wasn't a clever idea, but it wasn't what I needed. All I asked for was a round stick. With Dad's help, we could have had a fiberglass barge that slept six, powered by the lawnmower's gas engine. I decided not to ask Dad and told the guys we'd study the problem a while longer. Sometimes, a kid really just wants a round stick.

Our breakthrough was discovering several wooden

pallets behind my father's shop. Apparently, they had been used to transport bricks to the job site and soon would be returned to the lumberyard to recoup a security deposit. My epiphany was that a pallet, without any modifications, is also a readymade raft. All that remained was transporting our new craft to water, which proved more difficult than imagined. Constructed from pine 2x4s and lath strips, the pallet was not only sturdy but extremely heavy. Fortunately, our new raft could hold five because we had to recruit two additional kids to carry the fourth corner.

With only yards remaining between the water and us, mud covered our shoe tops as we slogged across the soft ground. With every step, we sank farther. We didn't launch the raft so much as finally sink so deep the pallet's bottom and the water's surface met on their own. More disappointment followed. Although The Pond had an immense surface area, its average depth was 6 inches and 18 inches at the deepest point. Shallow water combined with the weight of five sailors created limited displacement. In the end, our manned raft had a sailing sweet spot of 3 feet in any direction. No matter how vigorously we goaded the half-submerged barge with our bamboo poles, it wasn't going anywhere.

We spent the afternoon sitting on the raft in sullen silence. We sat long enough for sun to bake the gunk covering our clothes and skin. The resultant body glaze was immobilizing but at least it kept mosquitoes from biting. In fact, as the day wore on, I realized being a mud doll wasn't the worst thing in the world. The worst thing would be Dad discovering I had stolen his pallet. We should have toughed it out and dragged it home. If we just had hosed off the pallet and hidden it at the bottom of the stack, there wouldn't have been questions. Instead, the five of us took an oath to fake ignorance and vowed to retrieve it next fall after the water dried up. At that moment, we desperately needed lies that explained the wretched state of our clothes.

Although we didn't sail The Pond that season or even the next, my friends and I muddied ourselves at its edge for several more summers. When we were children, water had enduring seductiveness. Some things don't change. I went walking with my youngest grandchild yesterday. As she ran to greet me, she detoured four steps to avoid missing a puddle.

Kites

Neighborhood trees were still too small to be a problem but there were telephone and power lines everywhere. Those obstacles, in addition to towering TV antennae on every roof, made The Field the only place for serious kite flying. Kites I built were never too elaborate, generally constructed with twine, paste, newspaper, and pine strips bought from the hobby store. Cousin Chris once made an oversized box kite of red tissue paper. It was glorious, like something my dad probably built as a kid. Without disparaging Chris's mechanical prowess, I wasn't a huge box kite fan. They took two people to launch and were not very maneuverable. On the other hand, once airborne, box kites needed very little breeze to stay aloft.

Actually, it was cheaper to buy a kite than make one. Box kites at the dime store were 75 cents, but common, diamond-shaped kites were just a quarter. Sold unassembled, their paper came rolled tightly around the struts and secured with rubber bands. Packaged kites in the dime store bin were red, blue, white, or green, each featuring one of four (hidden) printed designs on the front -- American flag, rocket streaking to the moon, jet plane, or Flying Wing. All colors and illustration combinations flew equally well, but guessing the picture before it was unrolled added an element of suspense. A lucky day for me was pulling a Flying Wing, also known as the B-35 bomber.

Unless kites were damaged beyond repair (usually from being dragged or torn on shrubs), we didn't dogfight. Several of us walked to The Field together, but once the upper air streams caught our kites, flying was solitary play. We sat

Indian-style low in the wheat grass, and let the sun turn our faces and bare arms pink. We spent entire afternoons within speaking distance without speaking. Since a simple string tug corrected a meandering kite, there was ample time for minds to wander. Sometimes I sent messages to my kite -- secrets written on paper squares. By slotting the note, it could straddle the string and be pushed by the wind like a galleon's canvas sail. I remember the tautness of the string and how secure I felt being tethered to something so far from earth. I understand memories trapped in amber have disproportionate power, but there will never be enough days like those.

The Cowry

"It's not movin'."

"Shaddup."

"When's it gonna eat?"

Four of us were laying belly-down on Ronny Reynolds's driveway. With chins and elbows to the concrete, our bodies were arranged like spokes of a wheel and a quart-sized mayonnaise jar was the hub of our attention. Paul's view of the contents was obscured by label remnants, but Jerry and I could see fine. Air holes in the lid had been punched with a nail and water filled the jar to within an inch of the top. Inside the makeshift aquarium rested a leopard spotted cowry shell the size of my fist. Ronny's dad was Navy and they moved a lot. This was the second time Ronny had been through our neighborhood but we didn't like him any better this time around.

He was a bossy kid. Ronny was skinny, wide-nosed, and sported a blond flat top shiny with Butch Wax. Because his huge front teeth were gapped, he emitted a faint whistle whenever he spoke. Despite such personal distractions, Ronny could make the ordinary exotic. When on a roll, he was a carney. He told whoppers, but could be downright mesmerizing as he did.

This was the third consecutive afternoon we had wasted with Ronny and his jar. He claimed the cowry in the jar came from the Philippines, which had been his father's last duty station. I knew Ronny Reynolds probably was lying but it didn't matter today. Like Paul and Jerry, I'd been ensnared by his babble. Before Ronny's pitch, I thought my beagle was a pretty swell pet. However, just a few minutes earlier, Ronny had me toying with trading her for the jar.

I listened with my eyes closed, the way they make you listen to classical music in school. Unable to shut out all the brightness, the insides of my eyelids glowed orange. The sun's collected heat rose from the concrete through my T-shirt and jeans. The driveway's grit pitted the underside of my bare arms while the tops baked in the sunshine. The air smelled of sweat and hot rubber tennis shoes. As Ronny droned, my body slipped away. I was a denim cat napping in the sun.

"What do he eat?"

Ronny suddenly abandoned his lecture and addressed Jerry with condescension. "In the ocean these cowries eat water germs and seaweed or sometimes a fish. But here I give him special food I make myself."

"Will he eat this?"

I opened my eyes enough to see Jerry pull from a pocket a half-eaten wad of Wonderbread and peanut butter. As the youngest and always hungriest, Jerry filled his clothes with snacks before leaving the house. Even during games of tag or statues, Jerry clutched something edible with the intensity of a desert prospector protecting his canteen.

Ronny didn't appreciate it but Paul and I laughed.

"No, you little crap!"

"Hey! Don't talk that way to my little brother. Anyway, you know it's dead."

"Iznot."

"Izso."

That exchange continued until Paul and Ronny were forced to strike boxing poses. With squinting eyes locked and their fists idling, the big boys mumbled threats as they circled the jar. Their exaggerated movements were molasses slow as if they were dancing a manly tarantella. Before pride demanded someone throw the first punch, Jerry whined.

"Make it eat, Ronny!"

Being the oldest, Paul was first to shake off the impending fight. "Yeah, make it eat that *special food*," he spit, "or we'll know you lie."

Ronny lifted the jar from the concrete and hurried to his house. "Just stay put. I'll be right back."

"He's so full of it," Paul grumbled. "If it was alive there'd be pink stuff in it."

We were half way to the street before Ronny reappeared. "Hey guys!" he called, all friendly again. He set the jar down and pulled a lumpy square of paper towels from under his T-shirt.

"There we go," he announced as he unfolded the package for our inspection. Cowry food looked like crushed soda crackers and potato chips to me, but what did I know? Jerry impulsively reached for the food.

""I'll do it," said Ronny shoving him away. "This hasta be done right."

Ronny gingerly unscrewed the punctured lid and dropped in a pinch. Moments earlier, Paul had threatened to pound Ronny, but now he whispered, "Will it swim to the top?"

"Watch," was the smug reply.

The three of us held a collective breath, expecting the cowry to lunge at the bait but the shell didn't move. The surface food became waterlogged, bits sank in leisurely zigzagging paths. Soft globs of cracker paste imploded on the cowry like tiny depth charges hitting a disabled submarine. Still, the cowry didn't move. The jar soon was so clouded by food particles that it resembled a snow globe.

Paul finally said what everyone was thinking. "Ronny Reynolds, you're one big, fat liar."

Before that argument gathered steam again, Ronny pricked up his ears like a dog and addressed a voice we couldn't hear. "I'm here, Mom. I'll be right in!" After extracting promises we'd wait for him, he ran the jar into his house for a second time.

We were already to the street again when Bobby emerged. "Guys! Sorry you missed it," he said, thrusting the jar toward us, "but my mom needed me. Look! It ate everything!" Sure enough, not a speck of special food remained. The leopard cowry, apparently satiated now, rested in crystalline water that sparkled in the afternoon sun.

"Wow!" gasped Jerry.

"Can't believe you missed it but he'll be hungry later," Ronny offered, using that tone of exaggerated cordiality I hated.

Paul ignored him and grunted, "Let's take the dogs to the park."

When Paul said that, Ronny got crazy mad, waving fists and telling us never to step on his property again.

"You're such a liar, Ronny Reynolds. Come on, guys," Paul ordered.

"Sure. Go on you rats! I had a professional collie and she was way better than your mutts. Smarter than Lassie, too. Once I had a blue parrot who knew a hundred French words!"

We left Ronny clutching his jar. I tried not to look back but his sobbing was disturbing and irresistible, like a freeway wreck that makes drivers slow down and rubberneck. Tears cut through the dirt caking his face, spit flew and his gapped teeth whistled, but Ronny Reynolds mattered less with every step I took.

Doggone

When our son first married, he and his bride tried to pacify us with granddogs instead of grandchildren. For a long time geezers have turned little dogs into replacement children, but it's fashionable among young couples as well. If dressing dogs and traveling with them in public was an accurate indicator of how well they'll raise real children, most couples would be sterilized by the State. Fortunately, when predicting the likelihood of successful parenthood all bets are off. Our kids were terrible with thoroughbred wiener dogs, but grew into game and energetic parents. Actually, no one is prepared for the tsunami called *children*.

After the first human grandbaby arrived, the kids' house suddenly was too small to share with dog siblings. Consequently, our granddogs moved to a farm in the country. No, they really did. Actually, it was a ranch and not a farm. Our daughter-in-law's folks (the *other* grandparents) generously adopted the animals but had no illusions about converting two wiener dogs into working stock. The arrangement worked well since the granddaughter was able to enjoy pets during her frequent visits without the attendant responsibilities and complications. It was all rather idyllic until the child turned five. A darker side of country life revealed itself when a marauding coyote snatched one of the tiny dogs.

My wife and I promised to be sensitive and note any signs of distress during the child's next visit. It was agreed it would be best if she talked it out rather than bottle up her feelings. We were relieved when she broached the dog's death herself. My wife peeled vegetables at the sink as our baby girl sat atop the kitchen counter watching and talking.

"You know what, Grandma? Bozzie's gone."

"Gone? What do you mean?"

"He's not here," she whispered, shaking her head.

"Where is he, Sweetheart?"

"He's up there," she said blankly and pointed skyward in explanation. "Not in the ceiling," she struggled to clarify, "but ...you know...in heaven."

Animal Farm

Animals weren't fashion accessories or surrogate babies in my old neighborhood, but wherever children were, pets happened, no matter how fleeting those relationships. Predictably, our parameters for acceptable companions were flexible. If adults couldn't provide pups and kittens, we domesticated toads, ladybugs, and injured birds. We had less desire to dominate another creature than simply share space with it. Even a grasshopper was worthy of a shoebox diorama with grass cuttings to eat and a Kleenex bed.

My family made room for many transient pets, like carnival chameleons, guppies, mail-order sea monkeys, and those dyed Easter chicks sold in dime stores. Once we even had a tortoise. That acquisition occurred during a road trip to Bishop when Dad (uncharacteristically) stopped to aid an inattentive desert tortoise destined to become road kill. We expected he'd carry the creature to safety across the highway. Instead, Dad threw the distracted reptile into our car's trunk. With a power tool at home, he drilled a hole in the shell's overhang big enough pass heavy cotton string through. His plan was to tether the tortoise to a wooden ground stake, figuring it would have enough freedom to forage the backyard while remaining ours. A week later the stake remained but 100 feet of string and the tortoise were missing. Whether Lightning engineered his own escape or had an accomplice was never established.

Of course, there wasn't a shortage of traditional pets like dogs or cats, but neither was there a Lhasa Apso or hairless Sphynx among them. Most were offspring of other mutts on the block, much like the kids who loved them. My first dog came from a pet shop. She was a beagle I named Nancy (after Sluggo's girl in the comics). I didn't have Nancy very long before she was put to sleep to appease some lousy adults. When riding past our house, their bike-riding brat made a habit of kicking Nancy in the face. Naturally, the dog finally lost it and nipped the girl's ankle, barely breaking the skin beneath her thin cotton socks. Maybe that's why I still associate dog ownership with excessive drama. Probably that injustice made me a cat guy for life.

My parents tell stories about cat named Smokey, a family

pet before I was born. They made him toys for chasing by crumpling cellophane wrappers from their empty cigarette packs. Eventually, the cat was so conditioned by this ritual that no one could smoke inside without being stalked by the impatient feline. The mere suggestion of lighting up resulted in surprise attacks by a leaping Smokey who could slap the cigarette pack from a guest's hand in mid-motion.

My first cat was actually a secondhand one. Fluffy, a longhaired Persian, originally belonged to Grandma. Since my dad's parents lived only a mile from us on Citrus Avenue, we visited quite often. Apparently, at two and with no pet of my own, I was quite smitten with the fuzzy diva so Grandma sent her to live with us.

By then, Fluffy was no kitten and lacked the patience to deal with children. However, B&W photos suggest we managed a tenuous truce at some point. In a favorite family snapshot, I am lying on the floor watching TV. Fluffy sits high on my shoulders grooming my head. As she drenches my hair with more strokes of her sandpaper tongue, I indifferently suck my thumb. With my free hand, I use the cat's bushy tail like a feather duster, flicking my nose and chin.

Such Kodak moments aside, Fluffy never adjusted to her changed station in life. Staying with us represented a long fall from the egocentric luxury she experienced at Grandma's. My sister was born when I was three. The day my folks carried Diana through the front door; the cat left by the back door. We scoured the neighborhood imagining all sorts of terrible fates but discovered Fluffy living on the street behind our property. She had taken up with the Pomegranate Lady whose house was at the base of Suicide Hill, so she probably wasn't homeless for more than an hour.

Truth is, Fluffy had the yes-the-world-revolves-around- me aloofness that makes cat-haters froth. But that's just the way some of them are made. For Fluffy, living in the shadow of one child barely was tolerable but sliding farther down the totem pole was unacceptable. Plainly, things weren't going to improve so Fluffy cut a better deal. Naturally, we dragged the cat home and eventually she quit trying to escape. After a few months she could even slink by the baby without hissing.

It took another three years but Fluffy's psyche healed enough she seemed her old prissy self. Then Brother Frank was born and Fluffy moved back with the Pomegranate Lady for good. I remember when Frank was older and we played together on the backstreet. Some days, especially when trees surrounding the old woman's house were losing leaves, we'd catch sight of Fluffy in a window. I'd tell my disbelieving brother that the beautiful gray Persian actually belonged to us. I'd call her name and throw pebbles at the glass to catch her attention, but Fluffy just stared through me.

Pete The Cat

Although our neighborhood was ripe with young playmates, my little brother never needed other children to be happy. In fact, one of young Babe's earliest and best friends was Pete the cat, a stray who adopted us. If Pete hadn't taken the initiative, we certainly wouldn't have because Pete was one ugly cat the night he came to stay. He announced himself by hanging onto the center of the front door screen, throwing his head back, and emitting a cry like an in injured infant. We kids rushed to the window to see what the matter was. The cat was thin but full grown and Pete's black coat was so badly matted that Mom knew he had mange. She patiently explained the animal should be left alone but we begged to let him in. Of course, if there were a wounded rhino on our porch instead of a cat, we would have made the same passionate pleas.

For reasons unknown, Mom relented and told us to stand back, that she'd deal with the cat. As threatening as the animal looked, once comforted, Pete proved to be one of the gentlest creatures God ever made. He was not diseased; he just needed grooming and food. Pete became Babe's pet not by formal agreement but because their temperaments meshed. The cat was as easygoing as his master. Frank carried Pete around the house and yard draped stole-like around his neck or supported on outstretched arms like a charcoaled Yule log. Over the years, his ways of toting the cat permanently stretched Pete's body length by several inches. However, if Babe ever hurt him, Pete seemed to understand it was unintentional. In any case, the cat gratefully accepted love without complaint and this boy and his cat grew inseparable. As could be asked about all great friendships, who chose who?

What She Would Have Wanted

Maggie was our cat for 18 years so all the children have history with her. When the granddaughters were 5 and 8, Maggie slipped into a brief bout of cat dementia before running down like an old clock. During Maggie's final week, she sought out a dark closet in the spare bedroom. Although she refused food and water, the cat wasn't in obvious pain and responded to our touch until the end. Still, watching her wither broke my heart.

My wife decided it best the little girls understand that Maggie was dying before they visited. So while I drove and they listened from the backseat, I gave my best speech about the sacred companionship of pets, the importance of honoring their passing, and taking comfort from the promise of a better place in the afterlife. I thought I'd done a pretty good job so I was unprepared for their prolonged silence afterwards. I was already mentally berating myself for being unnecessarily morbid and heavy-handed when the littlest one spoke up.

"Pop-Pop?" she whispered.

"Yes."

"Do you know what you should do when Maggie dies?"

"No, Sweetie, what should I do?"

There was another long pause.

"You should buy a monkey!"

"Yeah," her older sister chimed in, "monkeys live to be 40 years-old!

According to the parents, our girls had been pursuing their monkey agenda unsuccessfully for two weeks. Obviously, they considered Grandma and Pop-Pop easier marks. I admired the little one for seeing her shot and taking it. Since my motto concerning grandchildren is "do whatever they say and no one gets hurt," her plan had merit.

CHAPTER 5

Spending It All

Stroll

If I walked 7th Street to reach the stores, I either planned a library detour or hoped to catch Tina playing in her front yard. Rarely has a name fit a girl so perfectly. She was Tinker Bell incarnate, but she was always trying out nicknames. During fifth grade she wanted to be *Tiki* because necklaces with pendants of Polynesian gods were all the rage. I called her Tiki that month. Tina or Tiki, I doubt she ever knew how often I thought about her.

If my buddies and I were walking to the stores, we'd stop at a Schwinn bicycle shop across from the library. Of course, the clerks knew we weren't serious shoppers, but occasionally saved face by pooling money for 25 cent decals kept in binders on the counter. Actually, they had the best collection of flaming skull and Rat Fink decals anywhere. The shop also carried a small inventory of Revell and Hawk plastic models kits as well as the entire line of Duncan tops and yo-yos. As official distributors, the traveling Duncan Yo-Yo Man performed exhibitions there several times a year. The demonstrations were free and we always picked up a new trick or two. If I had been any good at assembling models, I also might have won a ribbon in the store's monthly contests and had my creation displayed in the front window.

Home Of The Flying Red Horse

A Mobile gas station and Rexall drug store served as bookends for the two-block row of storefronts. My dad patronized Mobile because he had their credit card. Kids stopped there to fill bicycle tires or buy patched automobile inner tubes for a dollar. That was cheaper than renting a tube at the beach plus you got free air. The gas station's soda machine also had a good selection but unless you wanted to pay a bottle deposit, you had to drink it there.

As kids, we didn't regularly shop every store, but at one time or another we entered them all. That was because merchants gave away tickets to movie matinees at the Palm. It was a summer sales promotion that required no purchase, but tickets were limited and you had to ask a clerk for one. With movies as incentive, I once found enough courage to enter a shop with ladies' underwear in the window.

Got One Of These?

There wasn't much at the hardware store that intrigued me, but as I grew older Dad sent me there on errands. Customers were different than those at my father's lumber company. Most likely, these men handled tools only on weekends and it showed in their demeanor. Obviously perplexed, most wandered holding some random part, hoping to find its match somewhere among the aisles of endless bins. I felt right at home. Actually, I best liked watching the machine that shook paint cans and always slipped color sample cards into my pocket as I left. Once the paint department gave away bud vases. To publicize their vast selection of colors, a clerk swirled white bisque vases on a stick in a deep pan of multi-hued paints. Cool.

Toy Store

The shopping center's west end also housed businesses selling liquor, furniture, jewelry, and even a cubbyhole that shined and resoled shoes. However, the only store in that wing that mattered was the toy store. If a kid needed simple things like a horseshoe magnet or a balsa glider, the dime store was fine. For anything unique like wax dinosaurs or an ant farm, the toy store was our only option. Problem was, the man who owned it hated us. To me, he looked like Sidney Toler in his Charlie Chan makeup.

The toy store man was big and hulking and wore a white smock like a pharmacist or barber. When he had no customers he stared blankly out the front display window, pressing the tips of his fingers together like a spider doing pushups on a mirror. If an adult accompanied us, the toy store man was sickeningly solicitous. When it was just us kids, he demanded to see our money before letting us into his store. Even after proving we had cash, he directed us to sections with toys we could afford.

Groceries

An upright pig wearing a butcher's cap and apron seemed a surreal mascot for a grocery. I guess it was no stranger than painting their storefront pink. I considered groceries minimally more interesting than hardware, but Piggly Wiggly added a lot of excitement to our lives. They sponsored elaborate mechanical rides for us in their parking lot, like a rocket ship that held 20 kids at a time inside and simulated flights to Mars. Foremost, the grocery sponsored regular visits by the Wienermobile. It was a great Saturday whenever Oscar Meyer (a little person) appeared in front of our grocery and threw handfuls of wiener whistles at us.

Drug Store

Piggly Wiggly took up most of the shopping center's east wing. At the far end was a claustrophobic drug store with narrow aisles and tall shelves. We never visited the prescription counter, confining ourselves instead to penny candy bins up front. The cash register lady, who also tended the candy, was protected by display cases of smoking paraphernalia like pipes and lighters; even selections of pocketknives, nail clippers, and wallets. One Christmas, I bought a Zippo lighter there for Dad that he really liked. Its see-thru base held the lighter fluid and had a feathered fishing fly in it for decoration.

There was a lot of merchandise stuffed into the very small store but our interest was candy. The clerk seemed to understand how difficult it was to concoct a perfect mix; choosing the best penny candy from wax lips and moustaches, Pixy Stix, Smarties (made in Great Britain it said on the wrapper!), Lik-m-ade packets, and all. Situated between Piggly Wiggly and the drug store was a dime store (for toys and film processing), a two-chair barbershop, and a variety store interesting only to women. Once, for a whole week, a blind man set his sidewalk business in front of the ladies' store. We didn't need the pencils he sold, but my friends dared each other to buy one. I never had owned a 50-cent pencil before. It felt strange when an adult, even a blind one, said he trusted me to pay what I thought was fair.

At The Movies

The Palm Theater, with neon palm trees above its marquee and Palm Avenue address, was hallowed ground. Family movie outings were limited to biblical epics shown at the Big Sky drive-in. Thanks to free merchant passes, however, I enjoyed many classic films without family. Since the time I had to leave the movie early and walk my sister home because Bambi's parents got killed in a forest fire, I preferred seeing movies alone.

Free seating for matinees was first come, first served, but they packed the theatre beyond capacity, figuring there'd be more customers for snacks. They even put kids in the smoking rooms at the rear of the auditorium. Those seats were softer and the sound was good, but the dim red light and plate glass window separating us took some getting used to. Free summer movies brought kids from all over; kids not from the neighborhood. That made the experience like a few hours in another town or maybe a different country.

Ushers were more interested in finding smuggled candy and pop than making the audience behave. The theater wanted us to buy stuff there, which wasn't unreasonable. Not paying admission freed quarters for popcorn and soda, maybe

Necco Waffers or Jujubes if I wanted to loosen some teeth. My favorite candy bar was Abba Zabba. Sold only at the theater, it had a gaudy black and yellow checkerboard wrapper. A Negro girl once scowled at me when I slid my Abba Zabba and change at the cashier. Maybe the wrapper's cartoon jungle native with thick-lips and bone in his nose explained some of her attitude. At ten, I wasn't the only American with an underdeveloped social conscience.

Those rowdy three hour matinees contained lots of filler like ancient serial westerns and Buster Crabbe space operas, but also presented classics like *Creature From the Black Lagoon, The Blob, How to Make a Monster,* and *I Was a Teenage Werewolf.* Standing in a movie line with buddies was an opportunity for honing our intellectual repartee. As we waited for show time, I remember a particularly heated debate prompted by the theater poster for *Attack of the 50 Foot Woman.*

None of us were rocket scientists yet, but the consensus was an alien's growth ray affected only flesh. Ergo, after being zapped, the attractive woman on the poster would grow but the sheet covering should not. Imagine our letdown when whoever constructed a perfectly believable premise involving space aliens and naked women chose, for no reason whatsoever, to ignore the physical laws of the universe. *Attack of the 50 Foot Woman* wasn't a bad film; it just wasn't as titillating as hoped.

About the time my family left California, a competing shopping center opened on the other side of Palm Avenue. Mom was convinced Big Bear's food prices were better than Piggly Wiggly's. I was won over by their comic book selection. Big Bear stocked *Famous Monsters of Filmland.*

Carnival Apparition

There was a pie-shaped lot bounded by the intersection of Palm Avenue and the Silver Strand highway. Before a developer spread asphalt over it, the land was an incongruous wild place in the city we passed when driving to Coronado or walking to the beach. After being developed, the lot featured a chain restaurant where we ate orange sherbet after church with Grandma and Grandpa. Despite its name, Palm Avenue featured very few palms then. Instead, the boulevard was bordered by eucalyptus trees with bluish, pendant leaves and gray, peeling bark.

These trees provided my nearest experience with snowstorms in Southern California. I remember late afternoons when their flowers rode sea gusts and the sky churned with pink snowflakes, all backlit by the falling sun. These flower storms were portents of spring in a place whose temperate climate never varied. Spring mattered to me because it meant the Carnival would return. Once a year, for three nights only, it claimed that otherwise vacant triangle.

The carnival wasn't my parents' idea of fun, but I doubt they conspired to hide its arrival either. That would have been impossible with radio promotions and florescent posters in every store window. Besides, children could see it for miles. Carnival neon created a dome of light on the horizon that looked like Metropolis to me. Although we lived blocks away, at night I could hear the Hammer's screaming passengers, midway barkers, and rock music pushed through tiny speakers on wooden poles. Television had already made circuses too familiar, but a carnival was still mystical and vaguely dangerous. Like an apparition, it sprang full-blown from the earth, spun its magic, and disappeared before a fourth day made it ordinary.

Incredibly, my family nearly missed the Carnival when I was eleven. I realize now my mother feigned relief when Diana and I told her this was the last night and weren't we lucky to have found out before they left town? "Yes," Mother replied, "We are very lucky indeed!"

Dad worked in the shop that night but Mom promised to take us. In fact, it was her opinion we kids had acted so mature lately that she trusted us to explore by ourselves. She'd drive us there after dinner and pick us up two hours later. It was a great plan but we had only 4 hours to get ready.

Glass Pyramid

"Can we do the coin toss before we go, Mom?"

"Yes, Mother, may we please play the coin toss game? It's over there."

"I don't think so. We need to get home."

"But Mother," my sister implored breathlessly, "John and I have played but Frank didn't which isn't fair. It wouldn't take long and we have money, see?" She pried open Frank's fist to reveal a sticky quarter and nickel and then rapidly fluttered her lashes, looking like Bambi with allergies.

The Falcon was parked thirty yards from the game tents. Mom considered the runway's corner booth with its peaked, canvas roof and milling crowd. Then she stared at her watch and back at us. Diana still wore her plaster angel face. "Please, Mother, please. Can't we please?" I nodded dumbly in agreement although at that precise moment I was wondering when my sister developed her facility for ventriloquism. How could she speak so rapidly and clearly without disrupting that phony smile? Frank, typically, was oblivious to the whole conversation. Instead, he was intent on removing a swath of pink cotton candy from the right side of his head, which matted his hair and clogged an ear.

"Oh, be quick about it. Throw your money away if you must," Mom relented. "I'll have the motor running. I've got things at home to do!" With that faint-hearted permission, Diana spun and ran into the dark. I followed but was slowed by Frank. We quickly lost sight of Diana so I navigated by locking on the tent's pyramid roof. Inside the booth, clusters of bare, big-watted bulbs dangled on thick, black electrical cords that made the canvas roof glow softly outside like a bedroom nightlight.

As Frank and I snaked through grownups, we saw Diana motioning. She had claimed a spot in the tent and was mouthing instructions we couldn't hear. The deafening rain of coins on glass drowned her out. "The money, the money! Get Frank's money," I finally understood her to say. We stood together at the plywood counter. On a gray tarp, centered on the carnival booth's dirt floor, was an enormous pyramid constructed from variously colored glass plates supported by overturned bowls and tumblers.

The game was simple. The player whose tossed coin came to rest on one of the slick plates could win items ranging from stuffed animals to radios and wrist watches. Awards were determined by the position and color of the plate. Also, the greater the coin's denomination (dime, quarter, or half-dollar), the more valuable the prize.

"Mister, we need three dimes for this quarter and nickel." At 7 PM Diana tossed the first dime. At 7:06, we were broke and trudging to the car. Just as Mom predicted, we threw away our money in very short time.

Mom seemed relieved when we returned, but vexed about how this evening was dragging on. She had every right to be miffed but she played along. I guess we were too adorable with smirks and hidden surprises behind our backs. Motherly love would be rewarded in a perfect world. Sadly, the world has never been fair.

From the car she coaxed, "Did you win? I'll bet you won! Come on, let Momma see what you won." Unwilling to end the suspense and reveal the treasures earned so quickly and cheaply, we giggled in unison. Diana broke the stalemate.

"Aren't I lucky, Mother?" my sister shrieked as she revealed the baby rabbit behind her back. Before Mom could respond, Diana broke into loud laughter and cackled again, "Ain't we ALL lucky tonight?" On cue, Frank held up his new goldfish and I my baby duck.

Mom was dumbstruck. Then she became so emotional over our family's collective good fortune that, I swear, her eyes filled with tears and she raised her hands to Heaven in a gesture of thanks. "We are all lucky," she sobbed. "I should say we are all very lucky indeed!"

Carnival Creatures

Winning the coin toss three times with our last three dimes

was the kid equivalent nailing the lottery's mega millions first time out. Parents bad mouthed carnivals, claiming they felt entitled to gyp people since they didn't stay around to face the consequences. I didn't know which particular carnival they were referring to, but my family now had three new pets for a 30-cent investment. That didn't sound too shady to me.

That night my sister wanted to wake the neighborhood and spread our good news. Mom just wanted us settled in bed. Considering the earlier chaos and the present late hour, the animals were allowed to sleep indoors. Frank put Goldie's small bowl on my writing desk next to his bottom bunk and I made Daffy a temporary house from a cardboard box. Mom wasn't certain a lining of old, soft socks and ragged washcloths would be warm enough so she suggested placing the box on the floor's furnace vent. In Diana's bedroom, another box housed the rabbit already dubbed Hoppity Hare, punning on Happy Hare, the name of a favorite radio disc jockey.

Diana kept Hoppity within arm's reach and fought sleep. Frank conked out in the middle of whispered welcomes to Goldie. Even my duck's needy peeps grew less frequent until it finally slept, too. But I was wide-awake. I couldn't stop the carnival sounds and lights inside my head. In dreams I shaped an elaborate duck pond I'd start digging in the backyard tomorrow. I wondered if they'd let me plant some weeping willows and how I'd get Dad to build a waterwheel.

The Duck And The Hare

I can't know what Mom thought about that night, but it must have crossed her mind the carnival menagerie were only temporary guests. Our track record with baby animals wasn't good. We had already loved to death our quota of Easter chicks and variety store turtles with painted, soft-shelled backs. Most likely, Mom was resigned to letting us enjoy them now and prepare for the animals' tragic but inevitable demise. On some future morning Mom would, as she had many times before, hold us and tell us of animal heaven. She'd help bury their earthly remains in a flowerbed along with our sorrow. Every death is significant but nothing rends a heart more savagely than the passing of anyone or anything loved by a child.

Predictably, Goldie died first because Frank was too young to understand a fish doesn't need three squares a day, much less the snacks they shared watching TV. Incredibly, the duck and hare beat all odds. Soon, Hoppity grew large enough that Dad built a hutch next to his garage. However, in spite of Diana's loving attention, the rabbit became so skittish that Hoppity only could be picked up by the scruff of his neck and even then would bite or kick with his strong back legs. Daffy remained a houseguest longest, but he also outgrew my room. Each day the duck's fluffy head inched closer to the box's top edge. When his newly sleek neck towered and bobbed above the box's rim and his flapping white wings tore at the cardboard seams, relocation was inevitable.

We moved Daffy to a wire pen angled between a garage wall and the backyard's redwood fence. Already too large for the bathtub, the folks assembled a vinyl swimming pool for us kids and the duck. Animals should be subservient to their human masters, but nobody explained that to Daffy. It wasn't easy accommodating the whims of a duck. With his monotonous honking, Daffy became the family alarm clock and feathered watchdog. When Diana and I released Daffy from his pen each morning, the duck circled twice in greeting and grabbed our offerings of breakfast scraps before waddling into the garden beds to search out snails.

In summertime, Frank liked eating his morning cereal at the redwood picnic table. Consequently, it became customary for Frank to end his outdoor breakfasts in tears after losing most of his milk and Cheerios to the duck. Although we really loved Daffy, that first summer with him was like enduring some bratty kid your parents make you play with because he's somehow related to you. Daffy didn't like his pen. He never wanted to be left behind. Still, he was a handsome duck and we created quite a stir when the four of us took our twilight, sidewalk strolls.

It's A Scrub

A week before school started in September, my family made a quick drive to Whittier to visit Aunt Betty and Uncle Don and their girls. Now, just 15 minutes from home, Diana wondered aloud about Hoppity and Daffy. Of course it would be good to see them, I thought, but I was concentrating on the model box in my hands. When our family traveled, each kid got to buy a small souvenir. There was a set dollar limit, but if we found something really special, our folks usually made up the shortfall outright or advanced our allowance.

It was past 11 PM but Diana and I were awake in the backseat. She was preening the black braids of her new Indian princess doll with beaded buckskin dress. My brother slept in the front seat on Mom's lap. This trip, Frank had squandered his choice on yet another fake Indian headdress made from dyed turkey feathers. He was wearing it now while curled in Mom's arms. Frank sucked his thumb and snorted as his free hand dangled over the transmission hump. A black rubber tomahawk slowly slipped from his grip.

Every time Frank squirmed, his feathers rudely brushed Mom's nose or raked her eyes. What a stupid kid. Although I negotiated a two-week advance, my model kit was worth every penny. It was Revel's version of the Redstone rocket that launched Explorer satellites. Frank snorted again and Mom sighed impatiently. By streetlight flickering through the car's side windows, I glimpsed the illustration on the sealed box. (Part of the agreement was I wouldn't open it until we got home.) Instead of a photo of the assembled kit, manufacturers used dramatic oil paintings. My model building usually resulted in sad, formless lumps of glue-laden plastic, but the cover illustrations were so compelling. Probably I should have left the kits unassembled and displayed the unopened boxes on my bedroom shelf.

I looked down. The fiery Redstone was frozen inches above its launcher. A yellow tractor/trailer that earlier delivered the missile to launch technicians was obscured by the rocket's billowing exhaust. *So beautiful.* Everyone was dressed in coveralls and looking skyward from a safe distance, their hands cupped like visors against their brows. *I looked up.* Suddenly, Dad's Chevy braked and lurched forward.

"Good to be home!" my sister announced like some airline stewardess addressing her departing passengers. Dad hadn't cut the headlights before Diana was out of the car and through the backyard's side gate. "I'm checking on Hoppity," she yelled as the rest of us shook ourselves awake and carried luggage inside.

I was at the dining table when Dad and Diana came through the back door. The overhead light was on so I could start matching trees of plastic parts with the kit's instruction sheet. My plan was to glue together at least the tractor/trailer before they made me go to bed. Dad and Diana were in the kitchen doorway. Dad's hands rested on her shoulders in a gesture more gentle than I was used to seeing. Diana stared at the floor and let her arms hang limply. She wasn't crying but obviously she had been. When my sister broke from his grip and ran to her bedroom, Dad didn't stop her. Instead, he bent down and spoke directly to me. "The hutch door is open and the rabbit's gone."

He also told me the duck was dead. From the way the pen was wrecked, most likely some neighbor's dog had gotten in. "Daffy was pretty tough but… Son, do you understand what I'm saying?" I think he expected me to cry or something but I didn't. I looked away from him and back at the box. I noted how my Redstone strained for the sky. How smoke and flames enveloped the buildings and people it left behind. I asked whether Dad had ever seen such a great rocket as this. And I told him to bury Daffy without me. I wanted no part of that.

CHAPTER 6

Fun with Dick and Jane

When Books Were Paper

Praising intelligence might be as empty as admiring physical beauty since both qualities involve the luck of genetics. But my mother was both smart and beautiful. In another lifetime, she would have finished college and entered a profession but that wasn't common then. In fact, the one neighborhood woman who earned a degree and competed elbow to elbow with men in offices was often the butt of snide speculation about her qualifications as a wife and mother. It's hard to look back without bemoaning unenlightened choices by other generations. Today we speak of the sacredness of individuality, yet millions still live stunted lives and society is blind to its culpability.

Speculation based on time shifting is fun (Would Michael Jordon be an icon today if born before James Naismith?) but we are defined by our own time. My mother believed books would improve her children's lives and she acted on that belief. Before we could read ourselves, she read to us. I remember a wartime set of Colliers Classics whose faux leather bindings came in rainbow colors. From the orange volume Mom first shared the poem, "The House That Jack Built." Years later, when I read "Jack" to my fourth grade class, it was an immediate and overwhelming success. In fact, it became our class's unofficial anthem. Much to Mrs. Nelson's chagrin, that year at least eleven other children presented their spirited renditions during Wednesday's Show and Tells.

Although our household was sometimes strapped for cash, there always were books. We had library cards, of course, but Mom encouraged owning books as well. More than once she filled my Scholastic Books order for school with change scrounged from her purse. A budget and a catalog with too many choices made planning the optimum order an education in itself. I liked Minute Mysteries and joke books and titles published in series because they looked cool bunched together on my shelf. (Possessing a complete collection of almost anything is still satisfying.) So great was Mom's belief in the transformative power of the written word that she knowingly let an encyclopedia salesman into our house. I think he got our address from the guy who earlier sold her Child Craft.

I sat on the couch between Mom and Dad as the World Book representative closed in for the kill. "If we buy these books you'll use them, won't you? They're very expensive." Before I answered, the salesman interjected he was offering the entire world's great knowledge for mere pennies a day. (Of course, that was a salesman's euphemism for five years of installment payments.) When I promised to read the whole set, my parents assumed I was excited by the prospect of acquiring the world's greatest collection of human wisdom. Truth is, I couldn't keep my eyes off one book's special section of acetate overlays. It was called The Visible Frog and by flipping the clear plastic pages I could strip the skin off a frog and see his guts and bones. According to the brochure, somewhere in those volumes were a Visible Man and Visible Woman as well. Would any boy need greater persuasion than that?

Mom believed a home library gave her kids an educational edge. Although paper books are low tech by today's standards, her desire was the same as loving parents who sacrifice for toys and DVDs called Baby Einstein, Baby Mozart, or Baby Bill Gates. It's an assumption marred by magical thinking, but motive is above reproach.

Repeat After Me

Elementary school's greatest gift was teaching me to read and write. Math? Not so much. I'm not saying mathematics is unimportant but unless one's job is developing optimal probabilistic seismic demand models for highway overpasses, for instance, most people need just enough ciphering to complete the morning Sudoku puzzle. Life's other math problems are readily solved with the aid of cheap consumer electronics. Anymore, not even clerks try to count back change properly.

After the rigors of kindergarten, I could print my name, count to 20 on a good day, recognize a stop sign, and identify most colors in the smallest box of Crayolas. All useful skills, but reading would be the life-changer.

Nobody got individualized instruction during elementary school. Parents taught children one-on-one, but public school instruction was en masse. Whether the skill was long division or swimming, one instructor demonstrated while 40 students did their best imitations. The motto was *keep up or be left behind.* And that's when the public schools were presumably good. Social imprinting that resulted from those activities might explain how boomers can so prize individuality but share a predisposition for immense tribal gatherings. From Woodstock to Tea Parties. We long to be unique but our generation's earliest comforts were communal.

Reading, like everything else, was taught with an assembly line's mind-numbing efficiency. Using secret (but undoubtedly science-based) criteria, my first grade class was divided into four reading groups. Each cluster of otherwise interchangeable parts (us) was designated by a bird name. We were Cardinals, Blue Jays, Orioles, or Buzzards. The teacher assured us (and our parents) that groupings were random and without significance, but anyone who saw those designated Buzzards must have had doubts.

In some sense, groupings didn't matter because everyone was taught the same way using identical materials. Rather than sounding words phonetically, we memorized whole words, using texts with limited and repetitious vocabularies. Positioned near the reading circle was a wooden easel with oilcloth pages introducing the main characters from our book - Dick, Jane, Sally, et al. Each oversize illustration was rendered in the same pastel watercolor style used in the text. Character names consequently became the first words in our reading vocabulary. Admittedly, the process was tedious and the stories boring but sometimes it felt almost like reading.

Similar strategies were employed to teach handwriting and composition. Again, all together, we practiced endlessly with thick green pencils and sheets of blue-lined paper so rough they still had chunks of wood and bark in them. Our teacher insisted we write full pages about an assigned topic and only use words we could spell without help. Not surprisingly, early attempts sounded like the primers we read. *I like football. Football is nice. Football is fun. Fun. Fun. Fun.* Worse were the holiday poems she assigned. I remember weeping at the dining table late one night and being told I wasn't going to bed until I thought of a word that rhymed with Thanksgiving. Some days I felt like a B-movie monster that's hated because it's misunderstood. *No bad! Me want learn. Really!* Adults who blithely force children to run gauntlets they'd never endure themselves should not be forgiven.

Not every classmate shared my angst. Elizabeth was a Cardinal by birth. She gloried in her station as teacher's pet. Elizabeth was tall, olive-skinned, with a royal nose and pointed chin. She parted her brown hair down the middle but, because it was so thick and wavy, it wouldn't lie flat against her head. That made her hairstyle resemble an inverted *V* that looked, appropriately enough, like headgear of an Egyptian princess.

Elizabeth wore dresses to school as was the rule. Although hers were usually fancier than those worn by other girls, all styled similarly with high, cinched waists and layers of petticoats that made her lower half resemble an open umbrella.

Apart from her remarkable appearance, Elizabeth was also the best student in the entire first grade. She out-performed everyone in every academic category. She was the math wizard who did subtraction and addition as fast as the teacher could write problems. If the rest of us understood the concept of compound words (two shorter words pushed together), we might not have be as awed when Elizabeth spelled 10 letter words during class bees, but I doubt it. She had a brain.

Elizabeth rarely joined us kids for recess, preferring to study inside or do chores for the teacher. Some thought her snobby but I blame her parents for dressing her in patent leather rather than penny loafers. I wondered how it felt to be as effortlessly smart as Elizabeth until she confided she worked with flashcards every night. I was no Elizabeth by the end of first grade, but I could read and write. There was more to learn, but it would be icing.

Everybody Knows

Public school bashing as recreation is so widespread that today few people insist on evidence anymore. Everybody just knows. Consequently, any accusation of malfeasance is credible if delivered with enough loud indignation. Opinion equals fact and angry ideology trumps science every time. The public schools are a tax dollar money pit whose true agenda is social engineering and leftist indoctrination. Furthermore, the system is staffed by incompetent (humanist, agnostic, atheistic, liberal, socialist, America-blaming, communist, fascist, new-world-order, --- choose an adjective, add your own, or mix and match) "educators" protected from public accountability by tenure and unions. Everybody knows that.

Exaggerated, certainly, but reflective of commonly extreme charges thrown about nowadays. Oddly, research suggests that even the most severe critics of education in general often believe their own neighborhood schools and teachers are exceptions to the rule. The big picture is disastrous, but somehow schools that critics have actual contact with buck national trends.

During the 1950s, an era whose memory still makes some weepy with selective nostalgia, our public schools were the nation's great social equalizer. The relative calm of suburban, white-bread worlds like mine coexisted with segregated swaths of poverty and inequality.

As grateful as I am for the 3Rs, public education also stretched my neighborhood's boundaries. Even in those days, race and class changed by city block. If we weren't in classrooms together, kids a mile from my home could as well have lived in China. Years later, the military draft provided similar co-mingling.

The public schools of the 1950s weren't better, but they mirrored their times accurately. I have infinite sympathy for today's educators who by and large understand the art and science of teaching better than anyone, but are bullied by people who don't teach. Raising a stick constantly higher and beating the dog until it jumps over the stick is a strategy for limited success. It is a plan devised by someone who loves neither dogs nor children.

I'm sure some will call it heresy to say so, but not all of American's children will grow up to be rocket scientists. If you are of prime boomer age or order, review your old transcripts before rhapsodizing about yesterday's academic rigor. Compare those graduation requirements with today's exit tests, even at the primary level. Convince me that skill assessments and surviving a personal interview is a good way to welcome a child to kindergarten and the joys of lifelong learning. Although my 5 year old granddaughter's learning readiness was in doubt because she couldn't recognize a cursive *f* and wasn't sufficiently assertive in her preschool interview, she's currently doing well in the third grade.

There is a manic urgency permeating public education

today I never had to endure. If I were king, my first act would be to sacrifice test preparation sessions for more recess. I wonder when the bit of optimism and curiosity is beaten out of students in the name of standards. Education that insists on pre-algebra at age eight must be balanced with opportunities to be a child. I'd support reform that reinstates time for dreaming.

Still The One

One of many things I like about the grandchildren's school is the space devoted to art. There is so much student work it spills into the hallway, covers the walls and drips from the ceiling. Our girls are fortunate to always have been provided an abundance of craft supplies. Doing projects with Grandma and Pop-Pop was old hat before they entered kindergarten, so I shouldn't have been surprised during the first granddaughter's first open house.

Our girl was showing her work folder to the folks and Grandma. When I asked to see her artwork, she pointed to a corner wall and resumed her presentation. In front of me were 20 goldfish drawings. Nineteen were nearly identical renderings in orange crayon. The twentieth fish was covered in sequins, glitter, and feathers. I didn't bother searching for a corroborating signature.

CHAPTER 7

Grand Parents

Things

With so many of us boomers joining grandparent ranks, there's growing appreciation for the role, at least among boomers. My neighborhood was too new for multiple generations, but my father's parents lived a mile from us and we had cousins an hour away which was not the case with most of my friends. As a result, any sense of those grandparents is more balanced but still filtered through my needs. I was one of several grandchildren they loved. As a youngster, I never considered their personal flaws or the troubled dynamics of extended family. As an adult, I can read between the lines.

It seems disrespectful when memory reduces whole lifetimes into totems and a few sense-filled remembrances without context. I'm certain a therapist's couch could loose two hundred more pages for this memoir, but they wouldn't describe my grandmother as eloquently as the smell of lemon drops, for instance. Perhaps insultingly, my father's parents are maple furniture, milk glass, fuchsias, and a concrete garden frog. In fact, the best portrait of my grandmother exists only in my mind.

She sits in her early American living room with the matching hutch of glassware at her back, surrounded by grown children, their wives and husbands, and of course grandchildren. Although it's her house and only family are present, she's in full makeup and dressed to the nines because she's always in full makeup and dressed to the nines. Grandma is telling stories again, some old some new, each made longer by narrative detours and laughter. When she pauses to reach for an ashtray, rhinestones shimmer on her eyeglass frames. "Mother, tell them what you told Reverend Garrison the other day," Grandpa urges. "In just a minute, Dad," she says a tad dismissively. This moment is about her and Grandpa encourages it, as do we all.

Living with a tornado relegated Grandpa to sidekick at family gatherings, but I know that is not the bigger truth of their marriage. He was a different man by the time he was my Grandpa. Inside me now, his presence is a slow, deep voice.

Grandpa led prayer at family dinner like he led the Pentecostal congregation in hymns and scripture reading. Church was my grandparents' life but they also had time for dancing, which was the circumstance of her heart attack. Grandpa loved Ray Charles' "Born to Lose" and everything by Nat King Cole. "We'll Sing in the Sunshine" by that *good lookin' Australian gal* remained a favorite, although it sounded more pensive after Grandma's death.

Only when I was older and he was alone did I gain the slightest understanding of him. I'm sure the man I describe is unknown to his children or even other grandchildren, but this is the one my heart houses. Truth isn't in the minutia of biography; rather it hides among keepsakes and fragments of memory. My grandpa is humming to a radio song with his eyes shut. He inhales deeply again. The voice is raspy from cigarettes, but when he sings I hear tears.

Evergreen

My mother's parents lived far away in Washington State. Both had long since quit working and lived with a daughter. When visiting us, they stayed a month or more because air travel was expensive and arduous for them. Or maybe the longer visit gave my Washington aunt and uncle a break from caretaking.

They seemed so much older than my California grandparents. To please her parents, Mom served odd food like poached eggs and toast or cottage cheese scoops on lettuce leaves, topped with peach halves and sliced cherries --- recipes she never used otherwise. When they visited hot tea replaced coffee. Suddenly, dinner meant purple beets and liver. They even took over my bedroom and we had to watch the TV they liked. Their presence in our small house upset everybody's routine but they were easy to love because it was so plain they loved us.

Bringing little more than their brogues, my grandparents emigrated from Scotland in 1919. Grandpa had traveled alone to America four years earlier to smooth the way, but left to fight for Britain in WWI. When peace broke out, he returned to America by way of Canada on a ship from Liverpool to Quebec. This time he brought his bride, Grandma, and somehow ended up in Bremerton, Washington. Grandpa was employed there as a gardener or groundskeeper all his life and they raised three girls. That's about all the biographical detail I know.

I'm not surprised when people lose interest in their life's work after retirement. Too often careers are purchased with youth and heath and practiced long after inertia replaces delight. In contrast, my grandpa never stopped gardening, not even at the rest home where he died. I wish I could find whatever the flowers gave him. Grandpa flew to California to see us, I know, but his other mission was to steal as many plant cuttings as possible. Our neighborhood was easy pickings and he got whatever he wanted using just his charming accent.

The prize specimens, however, were in Balboa Park's public gardens where it was illegal to even touch the plants. No matter. His harmless Chaplinesque demeanor hid a larcenous heart. Grandpa had a lot of gall and quick hands for an old man. Cupping an open pocketknife, he could appear to innocently examine foliage while surreptitiously cutting a 3-inch slip with enough nodes for rooting. On the return flight to Washington, one of Grandpa's suitcases contained a layer of wet sand that sustained his pirated booty.

My grandma wasn't always in a wheelchair, but I don't remember her before the stroke. As her grandkids, we never gave her condition much thought; it was just a part of her, like height or hair color. However, the chair made her arrivals at San Diego's airport memorable. Society was not as aware of people with disabilities then. After everyone else deplaned, Grandma was unloaded from the tail end with the cargo. (She always joked they kept her among suitcases and caged pets the whole way.) When the men in zippered coveralls lowered

Grandma with their hydraulic lift, she clutched her coat closed with one hand and acknowledged gawking strangers with a queenly wave of the other. She was an impressive mix of dignity and self-depreciating humor.

Grandpa's appearance was just as notable because he always wore more clothes than was appropriate in Southern California. His wool suits, sweater vests, and baggy, front-pleated slacks recalled the disheveled, defiant elegance of European refugees in B&W photos. A thick moustache drooped beyond the corners of his mouth. Not even a felt dress hat could contain an unruly lock of gray hair. He kept a gold watch in one pants pocket and his tobacco pouch in the other. My folks were cigarette smokers but Grandpa's pipe was exotic in comparison, with all its ritual bowl-filling and relighting.

The only time Grandpa dressed less formally than long sleeves and tie was at bedtime, when he covered his nightgown with a bulky plaid robe clinched at the waist. Sometimes he wore a nightcap. On his feet were thick knit socks with leather pads stitched to the soles. Grandpa called them *mukluks*. From my pallet in the living room each morning, I heard Grandpa's mukluks scuffing the hall's hardwood floor as he shuffled toward the bathroom.

Grandma's wheelchair was too big for indoors so she

spent most of her day in an upholstered wingback just inside the front door. From there, she could see outside or watch television. Word puzzles and *Readers Digest* filled many hours, but a collapsible table allowed shared meals and games with Grandpa. Frank was small enough to climb into Grandma's chair without hurting her. Diana and I liked sitting at their feet when they played cards, trying to make sense of the scoring and inhaling sweet blue smoke from Grandpa's pipe. He used burnt wooden matches to replace lost pegs from the cribbage board. They liked having us near and amused us with embarrassing stories about our mom's childhood.

More than once, I overheard my aunts refer to Grandpa's temper and domineering ways. Apparently, he was a stern and often difficult father. The only tantrums I remember occurred when he couldn't attend to Grandma's needs. He'd berate her for hesitating or a misstep when he walked her to bed or the bathroom. He blamed Grandma when his own diminishing strength was more at fault. I suspect growing old with grace and dignity is a romantic impossibility perpetuated by people who are still young. I can't know the man he was before, but he liked the world very much when he held us.

Mail Call

For Christmas gifts, Aunt Anne and Uncle Lee sent my folks jars of pink, smoked meat from salmon they caught in Washington State. Often the box included seashells for me. Once Grandma and Grandpa sent us Japanese fishing floats. The hollow green and amber glass spheres ranged from six inches in diameter to more than a foot. They were made to suspend huge, twine fishing nets at sea but sometimes broke loose (probably during storms) and were carried for miles by currents until they washed ashore in Bremerton. The floats were beautiful and holding something from places so far away made me dizzy.

I've grown as absurdly dependent upon cell phones and electronic texting as anyone, but I use old-fashioned mail to say anything I want remembered. My Washington grandma taught me that. Long distance phone calls used to be awkward, quick, and expensive. By the time it was my turn to talk, I was left stuttering because Frank and Diana had used all the topics. Grandma couldn't be with me whenever she wanted so she sent notes and small gifts. When you receive an envelope or package with your name on it, there's no doubt you're important to somebody. "The Space Needle's elevator moves when you hold the pen upside down! I hope you like it." "This Brownie camera was free for drinking Lipton Tea. Please send pictures of you with your brother and sister." No distance is unconquerable. I never used the pen or camera without thinking of her.

Because my wife was raised as an Army brat, there isn't the same continuity of place and characters in her childhood stories, but there are the same recurrent themes. At the root of the sturdiest remembrances are instances when we were granted or denied what we needed most - protection, encouragement, love. In both of our lives, grandparents provided security and continuity disproportionate to shared time.

When she and her brothers were small children, their grandmother postponed cleaning windows after they visited, unwilling to remove their lip prints and finger smudges from the window glass. I'm similarly disinclined to retrieve the crayon or stray Lego left beneath the coffee table after my girls have left. Like an archeologist, I label all artifact drawings and scribbles with the date and circumstance of their creation before storing them in zip lock bags.

Parenting is difficult because you are discovering yourself while feeling simultaneously responsible for your child's well being and the happiness of your spouse. Grandparenting is less stressful. By the time grandchildren arrive, you either know yourself (or have given up trying) and your spouse has made herself happy (or is gone). The child you worried about is now the grownup and you are left to be your grandchild's coolest sidekick. Being a grandfather has taught me that a life lived in isolation is pointless, that growth is measured by connections. Even my wife, who is perfect by all reasonable standards, is never braver or more unselfish as when she loves her granddaughters.

Oval Portraits

The finale of all family gatherings was the dreaded group portrait. No sooner had women cleared the table's last dessert dish than one of the men appeared with the household camera. This ritual was so ingrained that everyone knew which sofa or wingback chair to gather around and in what arrangement. This lent a kind of interchangeability to an entire decade of photos that differ only in wrinkle counts, severity of receding hairlines, and the number and height of children.

When families had just a Kodak box camera with paper-backed film, memories were captured relatively quickly - strike a pose and don't move before the flash bulb pops. The availability of 35mm cameras with German and Japanese names after The War changed that. Family portraits were no longer amateurish *point and shoot* affairs. Now, every man with a 35mm was a budding artiste. These cameras' range of manual *f*-stop and shutter settings, variable film speeds, and interchangeable lenses created endless opportunities to make lousy photos very slowly. At our house, Brother Frank served as warm-up comedian while Dad fiddled with his light meter. After framing us in the viewfinder of his imaginary camera, young Babe would enthusiastically command, "Okay. Okay. Everybody get behind the chair and the wall and smell. Smell real pretty."

As technology advanced, our history was captured in many formats: B&W, unstable color prints which turned orange with the years, Kodachrome slides, instant but fragile Polaroid images, and the first home movies. Although somewhat rare when I was a kid, 8mm (and later Super 8) cameras became middleclass toys. Not only were the first movie cameras expensive, they required investment in a projector and screen. Even if one had the latest equipment, making home movies used to be hard work.

Early movie film was so insensitive to low light that filming indoors required supplemental lighting. Usually, floodlights attached to an already bulky camera supplied extra illumination. Since these floods were powered from a wall socket, the cameraman's range was determined by the extension cord's length. Nor was it helpful the light bar's combined candlepower was equal to the flash at Hiroshima that vaporized victims into wall shadows. When people in old home movies shield their eyes and run out of frame, there's a very good chance they weren't just playing around.

Home movie making presented other challenges as well. Early 8mm cameras held just 5 minutes of film. This discouraged lingering on any subject too long, especially if it wasn't moving in an entertaining manner. Recording everything in 30-second bursts made it possible to squeeze an entire year of holiday gatherings onto a single reel of film. These limitations also explain dead relatives' inclination to spontaneously dance inappropriate jigs or wave madly whenever a movie camera was near.

Like my father, I became official photographer when I had my own family. I made 35mm stills and VHS tapes of my infant son. By the time by first granddaughter arrived, I was still shooting 35mm film but had graduated to Hi-8 digital tape. In fact, I have her first two years of life on video, in real time. Today, I add to our photographic history but depend exclusively upon a digital point-and-shoot and watch my video on DVDs. I'm sure I'll be forced to master other formats before I'm gone.

Today, cameras are so omnipresent that it's difficult to capture anything candid or remotely upstaged. In that sense, video is better because a cinematographer can outlast his subject until pretense drops away. As far as still photos, I now have so many images it's proved cheaper to buy an external hard drive for storage than make prints for albums. I doubt my heirs will ever argue about who they were or what the world once was like because I've captured it all on film. Perhaps that's a shame.

Sometimes I'll ask one of the girls whether she remembers this or that. Often the answer is, "No, but I've seen the pictures." I'm curious how technology will change her memories. The childhood living inside me is kept alive by more than photos. My version is a composite of imaginative revisiting and reflection.

Even when the subjects are unknown to me, people in old photographs are fascinating. However, I display relatively few of the photos I've taken. Similarly, whenever I'm nostalgic, I revisit the same 20 or 30 minutes from the hours of video I've archived. When I photograph someone I love, the goal is capturing an iconic moment in harmony with my heart's sense of that person. That would be the truest picture of all.

It is easier for a child to comprehend abstractions like the solar system than fathom his parents were once children. I remember staring at ancient hand-tinted photographs my parents claimed were of them. That boy with the Prince Valiant haircut in a red wagon *could* be related to my father if I squinted. And the smallest of three girls standing in front of the barn *did* have a rounder, softer version of my mother's face. But try as I might, I couldn't hear them laugh or imagine them begging to play outside a little longer. If those people were really my parents, it was unthinkable they had ever failed or cried because they weren't good enough.

When I was young, my parents were benevolent giants. Now I am middle-aged and they are old. They live far away from me and farther from each other. Admittedly, they are frailer and their love for me is more complicated, but they were always giants. I have photographs to prove it.

And I Ask Myself, How Did This Happen?

The four-year-old has the gaze of a forensic pathologist. I'm trying to divert her attention because she's staring at my teeth again. We love this child but her frankness can be as cruel as it is accurate. Once she told my wife, "Grandma, you're old," but back-peddled when she read the hurt in my wife's eyes. "I mean YOU'RE not old, Grandma," our girl clarified, "just your SKIN is old."

Grandchildren stories are a good indicator you're listening to a baby boomer. Just as we were the first generation to discover sex, truth, and self-righteousness, we also are the first to recognize the unique joy of grandparenting. Despite an earlier, collective assertion that we hoped we'd die before we got old, most of my generation hasn't followed through. Consequently, there still are plenty of us around and things look mighty different from this side of the mountain.

And even though we trusted science and denial to keep us forever young, neither cosmetic surgery nor vitamin therapy has applied the brakes. Rationally, no amount of protest or voodoo can derail our inevitable end, but boomers keep insisting they are aging on their own terms. Current attitudes about child rearing veer wildly between intentionally childless unions and indifference toward multiple out-of-wedlock births. Also, very public pregnancy and adoption of foreign babies are fashionable. In contrast, my generation (once all rebels) seems absolutely reactionary. We may not have all been traditional parents, but we've enthusiastically embraced the role of grandparent. Maybe that's similar to the strategy used by flower children who called themselves freaks. Co-opting name-calling neutralizes an attacker's power; whatever you say we are, we are. Sticks and stones, Punk.

So the four-year-old is fixated on my teeth. She's been raised by younger adults whose laser straight teeth have been bleached to glow-in-the-dark degrees. Consequently, she doesn't know what to make of my jack-o-lantern grin and the discoloration. "What's on your teeth? Grandma has it, too." As I've said, there's no judgment in the girl's observations. I explain what fluoride is and how, in the olden days, they permanently stained children's teeth by putting too much of it into the tap water. Also, when she sees adults with spotted teeth, it's a good guess they're about the same age as her Grandma and Pop-Pop. It's like dating trees by their rings, I suggest, which strikes her as quite amusing.

To keep the conversation rolling, I consider flashing my smallpox scar but that would mean descriptions of mass inoculations in the school gym. And then her inevitable *why* would lead to polio and iron lungs, which is a burden too dark for this conversation. Besides, the ring analogy isn't very good. Trees are judged by their inside history but humans rarely are.

Until recently, I enjoyed the privilege that race and gender affords all old white men. Now there's a growing cognizance I'm losing myself. Sometimes those moments are merely wistful, as when a young waitress neuters this former stud muffin using diminutives like Honey, Sweetie, or Sugar.

Other times my escalating invisibility is more disquieting. I mean no disrespect when I say there are days when wrinkles diminish me as surely as numbers inked on the underside of a wrist. With these teeth and balding head, I am easy to dismiss. So miraculous is the resting child in my arms who sees through this old skin and reads my heart.

CHAPTER 8

Ruined Eyes, Mushy Brains

Peanut Gallery

We've discovered grandchildren are great audiences for photo albums nobody else wants to see, particularly when the children pictured are now adults in their lives. Once that interest is tapped, they want to know about books children used to read, the toys, and even favorite movies and TV shows. With the help of cable programming and DVD re-issues, our modern girls have become *Jeopardy* level experts on the TV adventures of *Superman, Annie Oakley,* and somewhat unexpectedly, early episodes of *Perry Mason.* I hadn't noticed the overabundance of sepia and gray tones that runs through all artifacts of our youth until the youngest grandchild asked in all seriousness, "Was color invented when you and

Grandma were kids?" No colorized *Flubber* movies for them. If it's B&W, they'll give it a chance.

Of course, the earliest television I remember was B&W. Even after sporadic color broadcasts began in the mid-50s, most households couldn't afford the switch. NBC showed *The Wizard of Oz* every Easter, but it was years before average viewers experienced the glory of Oz and RCA Color in their living rooms. A stylized peacock logo announced whenever shows were in *living color,* but the bird on our screen stayed as perpetually gray as those flying monkeys. We were metaphorical prisoners of Kansas then, only able to speculate about the peacock's tail feathers.

Childhood was an era when science promised solutions for every current or future problem. (Witness those *Weekly Reader* promises of jet packs for everyone.) Consequently, there was no shortage of con artists to satisfy our hunger for electronic age miracles. TV screen too small? Scientific magnifying lenses enlarged your television's viewable area to 16 or 17 inches! These Plexiglas lenses attached to the face of the set or dangled on brackets between the set and viewer. Some were even available with adjustable floor stands. One of the more farcical products promised conversion of your B&W television to color for $2.98 plus postage. That miracle amounted to a plastic film with three horizontal bands tinted blue, yellow, and green. When placed over a B&W screen, the tinting was meant to suggest the sky and ground colors.

I recall the earliest TV programming in San Diego was not full day. Or perhaps my family just encouraged outdoor play after school. Whatever the case, missing afternoon television was no sacrifice. Daytime scheduling was dreg like *The Liberace Show* and soap operas. Occasionally quality programming aired, like *Time for Beany* which used hand puppets to relate the nautical adventures of a beanie-wearing boy and Cecil the Sea Sick Sea Serpent. An artistic triumph. Not every television show from free-range days was so ambitious.

My grandchildren were incredulous to learn television is older than I am because so few things are, at least according to them. I have great fun ridiculing young people's obsessive relationships with their cell phones, but probably I was as bad with television. I certainly don't watch with the same level of absorption I did, but I still respond to its comforting white noise. Compared to other home appliances, the TV gets more use than my Belgian waffle maker, but the jumbo flat screen and 200 channels haven't made most current programming as exciting as waffles.

I have memories of evening shows the family watched together but, as television lost its novelty, family viewing became more fragmented and less inclusive. Frank and I had favorites like *Sky King* and *Sea Hunt* while Diana wanted *Ozzie and Harriet* because she loved Ricky Nelson. Dad liked some sports, especially boxing, and Mom chose quiz shows. Increasingly, the television stayed on for long stretches during the day, even when no one was in the room.

Despite the 50s' technological quaintness, television's freshness once added a sort of *and I touched the face of God* experience that's missing from entertainment today. As a result, my relationship to TV now is like that of a tailgater to the game being played inside the stadium. *There is proximity but no relating,* as Nichols and May once observed. Fortunately, nostalgia channels and video technology let me castoff weary sophistication and revisit the B&W world. My granddaughters are intellectually gifted (naturally), but recently they've become bewitched by a box set of *Wonder Woman* shows from the 70s. I intend to get them back on track by introducing Irish McCalla as *Sheena, Queen of the Jungle.* Now there's an Amazon worth emulating.

Fanner 50s And Shootin' Shells

I would choose my son remember me as a man strong and principled enough to walk through life carrying a big stick quietly, like TV's *The Rifleman*. I've been a *Rifleman* fan since I was a kid buying cap rolls to feed my gun. The rifle was a Mattel replica, but it looked just like Lucas's Winchester 92 carbine with loop lever for rapid firing. Lucas McCain, the Rifleman, had enough physical advantage, deadly skill, and tragic history to have been a successful bully. But that wasn't the way that Union Civil War veteran, widower, homesteader, and father of young Mark rolled. Lucas had to be poked with a stick repeatedly to get provoked, but when his righteous wrath was unleashed, oh boy, watch out. Not unlike another mild-mannered, bleeding heart who snapped one day and spanked some moneychangers in the Temple.

Presently, I am 5′8″ but rapidly shrinking, at least according to the DMV in Lake Worth, Texas. That I'm also balding is no surprise to anyone who's met me and is 5′9″ or taller. Also, at 230 pounds, the Centers for Disease Control and Prevention (CDCP) has ruled my body mass index (BMI) makes me employable by circus sideshows. On the outside, I have nothing in common with Chuck Connors (the handsome actor who played The Rifleman) but I share biographical similarities with the character. For instance, although I am not a widower, if my first marriage had continued much longer I probably would have become one.

Additionally, like Lucas McCain, I am a veteran of a war most Americans want to forget. (*Not* Reagan's invasion of

Grenada.) But most importantly, when Lucas and I were single dads, we shared an abiding protectiveness for our young sons. In both fiction and nonfiction, whenever pieces of our life are stolen so indiscriminately --- by whatever damnable means --- that which remains is treasure.

Regardless of strangers' understanding or approval, the McCain character lived by his code. Even when publicly bullied with ridicule and disrespect (a common plot complication), Lucas turned the other cheek that meant bad people foolishly underestimated his resolve. Lucas McCain never justified himself to anyone except son Mark, and even those explanations contained no hint of apology. Lucas never related his beliefs to Mark in any comprehensive form; rather, his philosophy dribbled out in short aphorisms over shared bowls of squirrel stew during five TV seasons. Still, Lucas's convictions made his actions predictable. Although his New Mexico ranch placed him far from civilization, he constantly risked his life for abstractions like social justice.

Lucas McCain's advocacy of individual liberty and personal responsibility suggests some might classify him as libertarian. I can't judge since my knowledge of libertarianism is limited to political tracts found in the waiting room of every dentist I've known. Similarly, although there may be a suggestive subtext, I can't vouch that Lucas was an objectivist.

Even Cliff Notes for *The Fountainhead* bored me. *Fountainhead* is the one fiction book your accountant or technical support guy owns, like every serial killer possesses a dog-eared copy of *The Catcher in the Rye.* Ayn Rand wrote novels for people who otherwise don't like or understand novels because artsy-fartsy nuance like characterization and ambiguity detracts from big ideas.

Lucas would agree with aspects of both philosophies (especially those tenets of self-reliance), but his willingness to sacrifice sets him apart. Fairly or not, objectivism often seems a baroque rationalization for selfishness. Although The Rifleman never expressed it this way, he couldn't be free until society's most vulnerable soul was also free.

Commonly, the most eloquent apologists for war as first option have never experienced battle firsthand. Conversely, champions of negotiated peace are found among the most scarred and decorated veterans. Since nearly every *Rifleman* culminated with McCain using his rapid-fire rifle to disinfect the streets of North Fork, obviously he'd never wear flowers in his hatband and sing odes to San Francisco.

In my conservative estimate, he killed at least 200 men in defense of liberty during the show's five-year run. Lucas McCain was no weenie. However, the difference between The Rifleman and a common thug is he only used force to blunt force, never for reasons of vanity or personal gain. Still, Lucas McCain as father shouldn't be given a free pass. Exterminating human vermin might provide some teachable moments, but meting out that kind of deadly justice in front of a child remains questionable parenting. (It makes me wonder about the state of social services in the Old West.)

The Rifleman never had a sequel or a reunion show, so what finally became of Mark McCain is speculation. Surely, psychological trauma resulting from weekly threats against his father's life as well as his own - to say nothing of witnessing his father's easy brutality - guarantees some lifelong anxiety disorders. Perhaps Mark recast his childhood trauma to become a Trappist monk or a gunslinger. (Or maybe a Trappist gunslinger like his father.) Applying today's standards, at the very least, Mark McCain would be job security for any frontier Freudian analyst.

So far, nothing in this convoluted monologue touches the reasons I liked TV westerns when I was a kid, and there were lots of westerns - *Cheyenne, Wanted: Dead or Alive, Lawman, Cisco Kid, Wyatt Earp, The Rebel, Bat Masterson, Bronco, Annie Oakley.* Honestly, those shows are still enjoyable but none have *The Rifleman's* resonance for me. Shot in black-and-white using odd camera angles and harsh lighting, I liked the look of the show. Because it was filmed on a soundstage, the exterior scenes featured obviously painted backdrops and sparse foreground props, which gave the show a surreal quality like bits from a Kurosawa samurai film. The tense, spare soundtrack of *The Rifleman* functioned as a Greek chorus providing dramatic context and punctuating the simplest action or dialog.

Like other TV westerns of the era, *The Rifleman* featured storylines about the father-son relationship. However, rather than depicting a boisterous, joyous man-world like the Cartwrights' Ponderosa, the McCain ranch resembled a compound or monastery. There is an air of loss permeating most *Rifleman* scripts that is both profound and undefined. Nonetheless, without women and social distractions on the McCain homestead, endless physical labor killed the characters' capacity to ponder much more than food, work, and sleep.

Despite Lucas's protestations, not all of his choices were best for Mark. At least subconsciously, Lucas used isolation and Spartan existence to keep his dead wife and battlefield nightmares buried. Without aggressive rehab, everything wrong with his existence eventually assumed the shape of strangers living outside the ranch's well-kept fence and the change they represented. Even Mark's hesitation to engage in certain conversations suggests a Stockholm Syndrome victim more than a hero-worshiping son. Accordingly, Mark knew not to speak of everything he learned or saw in town; he suppressed questions like, "Pa, what was Ma like?"

I couldn't always read *The Rifleman's* darker text. As a kid planted in front of the TV, it never occurred to me how tenuous the tether was between Lucas and Mark. I certainly didn't infer lessons about the inherent fragility of all relationships or the impossibility of refilling a cratered heart. Instead, when I was 8 years old, I understood and acted as a child. Once a week, I endured 20 minutes of narration for 5 minutes of climax when Lucas McCain restored balance to the universe.

Mimicking him, I celebrated the ageless struggle between good and evil. Although the outcome of my reenactments was never in doubt, the ritual was necessary. Practice makes second nature. With a box of Greenie perforated caps - 250 shots per roll - I restored a lot of order from atop the concrete stoop, my rifle blazing. I still love the smell of potassium chlorate sulphur mixture in the morning! Nothing else in the world smells like that. And to this day, even without my Mattel replica Winchester 92 carbine, I know life is best spent helping good to triumph, no matter how poor the odds.

Whether high art or low art, it's all a Rorschach test ratting out inconvenient truths about one's self. Memory is a similar hoard of inkblots. Sorting the named from the inscrutable tells more about us than anyone else should know.

Ward, There's Something Wrong With The Beaver

I remember real housewives like my mom and her lady friends saying snide things about June Cleaver. For them, watching a woman in high heels mop a kitchen while wearing pearls and a crisp, shirtwaist dress was akin to watching a dog walk upright - possible but what would possess any dog to try?

The Cleaver household featured in TV's *Leave It to Beaver* didn't resemble any I knew. First, there weren't any two-story houses with dormers and chimneys among the interchangeable ranch-styles in my subdivision. Our ceilings were too low for a chandelier like the Cleavers had. Unlike Ward, my father didn't have a book-lined study where he did paper work. Yards weren't defined by picket fences and the neighborhood was too new for stately trees and thick shrubbery. We had sidewalks like the Cleavers in Mayfield, USA, but ours didn't go on forever - at least not yet. They were under construction.

In a greater sense, everything was under construction in my mid-century existence. The physical neighborhood, as well as our lives, was a tabula rasa waiting to be scored. The native landscape was recast daily by men and machines. Hills leveled, canyons spanned, water diverted, gullies filled, roads paved, buildings built. Whatever made the world more functional and modern - those were tasks my father and blue-collar types embraced.

After purchasing temporary peace with their collective blood, the Greatest Generation (the boomers' parents) re-imagined the world without Depression, without war, and tried to forget their stolen youth. Society hungered for normalcy. Given that context, the Greatest Generation's almost psychic need for structure and conformity is understandable if not rational. Television's family sitcoms like *Leave it to Beaver* didn't create that longing for order, but they helped elevate family status while indirectly limiting its boundaries.

Most television families lived in vaguely Midwestern places like Springfield, Hilldale (Donna and Alex Stone's residence, not to be confused with Ozzie and Harriet's hometown of Hillsdale), Bryant Park, etc. These neighborhoods suggested history and moderate but comfortable wealth; the kind of lifestyle only possible after struggles by earlier generations. In other words, the middle class dream presented on television was still lifetimes away from our modest, working class reality in Southern California.

TV moms labored outside the home as a civic duty, not for money. TV dads worked in offices, cared about golf, and wore ties even when they relaxed. Try as he did, Ward Cleaver never looked convincing holding tools, especially when he tucked his sweatshirt into pleated dress slacks and marked his forehead with a theatrical smudge of oil.

With two parents and three children, my family slightly resembled television's ideal. However, the only way my father would have known anyone like Ward is if he built the Cleavers a gazebo. My dad would have been as hapless pushing paper as Ward would as a laborer. Although my mother revered cleanliness as much as June, she'd never wear her Sunday's finest to do chores. Similarly, Mom believed in community service like June, but worked through the Methodist church and not Junior League. We watched TV religiously in those days but no adult in my neighborhood had a prayer of becoming Ward or June. Like my parents, our neighbors didn't sleep in twin beds. They were destined never to live in a house that had more bedrooms than children. Still, most working families called themselves *middle class.* Just like the Cleavers.

Words and imagery have power beyond their simple denotation and conscious intention. In the largest scheme, *everything matters* even when the immediate effect is no more obvious than a water drop's abrasion against a stone canyon wall. Negativity like racism and sexism, no matter how humorously "innocent," can gain enough cumulative power to pollute national discourse and derail any hope of keeping America that shining city on the hill.

Because today's media proudly eschews any attempt at objectivity for displays of attitude, it's not surprising when pop culture archeologists attribute hidden agendas to all older media they encounter. Possibly I'm naïve but I doubt most 1950s television was conceived as manifestos espousing particular social and political dogma. It was another world entirely. Television's brainwashing reputation wasn't yet entrenched enough to earn the attention of evil billionaire ideologues intent on remaking the country in their own image.

At the same time, when taken together, those old shows offered persuasive (if often dishonest) arguments for the status quo - the way a choir transforms many separately mediocre singers into a single powerful voice. Family sitcoms from the 1950s are justly parodied for their abundance of platitudes, trivializing of serious topics, and ability to solve any problem in 30 minutes minus commercials. However, if they are nothing except heavy-handed marching orders for a bygone era, I don't understand why these shows have found a new audience among our grandchildren.

I'd guess *Leave it to Beaver* appeals to youngsters today for the same reasons it was popular when originally aired. The show's children aren't props or miniature adults. Family life is described from the child's viewpoint. Although not entirely absent, adult control over their kids' thoughts and choices is realistically limited. Ward and June love Wally and The Beav but don't keep them in protective bubbles. The boys are allowed to fail or succeed within the safe confines of a child-scale world.

It also helps that Beaver dresses, speaks, and reasons like the eight-year-old he portrays when the series began. (It's a bit disturbing; however, when five seasons later Beaver is *still* acting and dressing as if he were 8.) Portrayals of the Cleaver boys and their friends are starkly different from those by contemporary child actors. Today, many child characters are so precociously jaded they sound like strip club comics or players in *Bugsy Malone*. On the other hand, who hasn't known an insecure jerk like Eddie Haskell, a fair-weather friend like Gilbert, a weasel like Judy, or a loveable mutt like Larry Mondello? These characters are recognizable to audiences today.

Although plots were typically child-centered, *Leave it to Beaver* occasionally offered authentic takes on parenthood, especially in the earliest episodes. Even with a penchant for overdressing, June was surprisingly genuine whenever she tried to spare her boys emotional pain or expressed fear their childhood was passing too quickly. Ward played the usually stern patriarch but never with inflexible arrogance. Occasionally, he revealed unusual empathy by recalling unresolved childhood hurts between him and his own father. Ward projected strength and certainty in his father role, but intimated that confidence is often a façade.

Leave It to Beaver was just a TV show but inexperienced mothers and fathers in the 50s could have found worse parenting models. The Cleavers were engaged with their children but weren't their buddies. They enforced household rules together. They disciplined sparingly but consistently, expecting their sons to exercise self- control and judgment. When Wally and Beaver inevitably strayed, the boys made an honest accounting and tried first to right the situation themselves. Finally, the Cleaver household never ran on automatic pilot. You'd think life would be easier with your own theme music and a team of scriptwriters, but these entertainments contained an implicit reminder that real family life requires sacrifice and constant tending.

More than once my youngest granddaughters have wished aloud they lived in one of those *Nick-at-Night* neighborhoods. Ours are children who want for nothing materially, whose affections are courted by a large extended family. My girls achieve in exemplary schools and, at 6 and 9, are comfortable with cell phones, iPods, and the Internet. With plenty of paid lessons, camps, and fieldtrips, there is no shortage of enrichment. In spite of this (or because of this), exotica to them is catching frogs, being free to wander the neighborhood alone or spend time with fireman Gus like Beaver does. They call Grandma and I lucky because in the olden days we got to make all our own stuff.

When the girls stay over, we visit the requisite number of museums and an occasional Chuck E. Cheese. That's appreciated I'm sure, but we're learned they crave something simpler and cheaper - time to be children. The days they cherish are the ones most wasted; days structured by their own whims. It's unfortunate that trusting a child to educate and entertain herself is now a rare and revolutionary act. Today is wonderful but whenever the girls need, they know the way to Mayfield.

The Knob

One knob turned the set on and controlled volume, the other was the channel selector. Working class homes had one TV in those days and kept it in the living room. Consequently, if I didn't like what the parents watched, I found something else to do. Area programming was dispersed by transmitting towers and home antennae so we felt fortunate to have 3-4 watchable stations on any given day, barring storms. With no broadcasting satellites or fiber optics providing high quality service under all conditions, men turned to mass-market magazines like *Popular Mechanics, Popular Science,* or *Popular Electronics* for technical support. Coaxing peak picture quality from a 12" Zenith tabletop was an ongoing national obsession and hotly debated wherever men gathered. The number and variety of rooftop antennae that formed our neighborhood skyline were evidence that everyday Yankee ingenuity was alive.

Old people and amateurs believed claims made for those silly, telescoping rabbit ears that sat on top of the TV. Real men knew the only answer to reception problems was size. The brand of television antennae wasn't as important as the height of the pole it was strapped to. Sometimes antennae were planted freestanding next to the house (which made adjustments easier) but generally mounted on the roof and stabilized with guy-wires. The aim was to install the tallest antennae possible, short of attracting undue lightning strikes or impeding local air traffic.

In those days, the slightest change in atmospheric conditions affected picture quality. As a result, three or four times a week Dad planted himself on our roof to adjust the television's directional antennae. It required the whole family to achieve immaculate reception. Dad turned the antennae pole, Mom judged picture quality, and we kids were the "telephone line" between them. Men straddling roof peaks and screams of "Better. Better. Worse!" coming from open windows were so common as to be hardly noticed. Then it wasn't unusual to miss the first 5 minutes of the *Red Skelton Show* because of cloud cover.

Owning a television was a status symbol, but buying luxury items wasn't the only route to status. For instance, owning a backyard barbeque was enviable but building one from bricks earned special recognition among men in my neighborhood. One of my father's first home improvements to our tract house involved television. Dad set the local DIY bar impossibly high with a media center that encased both sides of the wing wall separating our living and dining areas.

There was a television screen and cloth covered speakers on the living room side. On the dining side were an AM radio and the household's only telephone. (The phone was the black metal variety whose heavy electro-magnets made it impossible for children under 5 to lift the receiver without assistance.) The third elevation facing the pathway to the kitchen featured a 10-gallon tropical fish tank. Dad pulled together these disparate design elements with a wraparound planter filled with real devil's ivy and arrowhead vine, at least until they died from lack of light and were replaced with plastic.

Anticipating his sophisticated creation would require future maintenance; Dad mounted the naked television chassis to a sliding shelf with casters. This made the TV screen flush with the cabinetry but kept the circuitry accessible. The radio on the dining side was built into a camouflaged hinged door that gave complete access into the belly of the beast. Still a toddler, I discovered peace in that dark place, comforted by the hum of an aquarium air pump and the orange glow of vacuum tubes.

As I've stressed, my father was (and remains) an example of his generation's exceptional craftsmen who bordered on artisan. Although he (like DaVinci) often lacked the financial resources to give his visions ultimate expression, in many ways the 1950s suited my dad. First of all, it was a period of great optimism. Secondly, skills men like my father needed to improve their lot were mostly ones they'd been honing forever. Whatever tweaking their education needed could be found in a manual or an apprenticeship through a union. Finally, there was opportunity.

It was a time before the richest few needed it all and

middleclass dreams could be purchased with virtuous hard work. When life is ascribed a mechanical predictability as it was during the 50s, pathways to happiness were also methodical and uniform. Then it was easier to believe a man's success or failure is completely his own making.

Don't infer from my father's media center that he loved music and movies. In fact, he really wasn't much for passive entertainment and could hardly sit through an hour of television. He was most engaged when the screen went blank. Then he plucked parts from the TV's guts and ran them to Piggly Wiggly's tube tester machine. That is an obvious pattern of my father's life – his joy is process.

Although a fine photographer and skilled darkroom technician today, his fascination remains problem solving more than the subjects of his photos. A shade tree mechanic since teenage years, Dad lost all enthusiasm for cars in the late 1970s, when carburetors disappeared and new plugs had a life of 100,000 miles. The father of my youth was not an anomaly. Back then we had a family friend named Mel who spent hundreds of dollars and hours building hi-fi components from scratch. To premiere his handiwork, Mel chose stereo demonstration records rather than Beethoven. For 30 minutes, he regaled us with passing trains and balls bouncing from massive left speaker to massive right speaker.

CHAPTER 9

No Fair!

Polio

I've heard my granddaughters refer to elementary schoolmates using the jargon of counselors and social services. They toss tags like autistic, ADD/ADHD, OCD, and LD as if they were nicknames. Perhaps they don't understand the stereotyping that accompanies labels like those, but it's a more nuanced way of considering people than we used. When I was their age, children were good or bad, smart or dumb, friend or foe, and kids with special needs didn't attend our school.

That's probably why the polio kid sticks in my memory. He was around throughout my third and fourth grade years. We never shared a classroom but he was hard to miss. Even though the whole length of his legs was caged in metal, he never accepted help. Unless you were a girl, he could be pretty mean if you dared to make things easier for him. After awhile, kids learned not to hold doors open or empty his lunch tray.

He didn't walk so much as drag his dead legs. After balancing upright with crutches, he'd thrust forward one leg and then pull his whole weight to that hard-earned spot, just to repeat the process with the other leg. Polio Kid was considerably smaller than most of us and always dressed in clothes too heavy for the weather. Only his hands and face were ever exposed to direct sunlight. All his plaid shirts were long sleeved and most were western cut. Often a paisley kerchief was tied around his neck, but he also liked bolo ties. Among his favorite bolos was a stylized, silver thunderbird with nuggets of turquoise stone and another featuring a black scorpion trapped in a Lucite oval.

The polio kid wore the same heavy boots every day. They were brown and tightly laced. Because metal kept his legs from bending, his blue jeans were cuffed and perpetually stiff. He slicked back his black hair and tried talking tough like he was someone else. No matter, his girly voice scared no one. Polio Kid's general immobility, coupled with the unnatural roundness of his face and too many teeth, evoked one of ventriloquist Paul Winchell's dummies more than a cowboy or a schoolmate. As I said, he was there for all of my third and fourth grades. Early during my fifth year, his crutches were traded for a wheelchair. After Christmas, no one saw him at school again. His name was Raymond but he wanted to be called "Tex."

I Stand Accused

I've tried to recall details about my second grade but not much comes; not the layout of the classroom, nothing learned, hardly anything. I can't conjure the teacher's face, much less her name. Her disembodied voice is badgering and self-righteous. Mine is the kind of memory lapse associated with alien abductions and head trauma victims.

What I can remember about second grade is being falsely accused of robbing a classmate with a broken arm. The truth is the kid was using his cast to club some first graders in the sandbox. He also claimed my two friends and I stole the foil wrapped quarters stashed in the gap between his wrist and the plaster wrapping. More likely, the coins fell out when he was chasing people on the playground. All we did was stop him from hurting anybody and he ran off crying.

Back in the classroom after recess, everyone got out pencils in anticipation of the next worksheet. Instead of starting the lesson, the teacher gave a lecture about fairness and responsibility. The rest of the class was confused but it was obvious she'd heard how my buddies and I saved those first graders. I felt my face redden at the prospect of being singled out for praise. Then, in front of everyone, she charged all three of us with picking on the kid with the broken arm.

When we denied it, Teacher told us to be quiet and chided us for our cowardly actions. Then she forced us to apologize to the class for something we never did and sat us outside the classroom door. "Until I can stand to look at you," was how she phrased it. At home, my parents believed me but wouldn't make the teacher hear my side. Mistakes like this happen, they said, but Christians forgive. They also insisted I'd eventually re-earn my teacher's trust if I were doubly good every day. I don't think that ever happened but, like I've already said, I don't remember much about the second grade.

Running In Place

It was unfortunate that Mrs. Gardner, my delightful 3rd grade teacher, was saddled with students like us with waning enthusiasm for school. She couldn't compete with kindergarten's novelty or the excitement of first grade's initiation into literacy. By design, 3rd grade wasn't for quantum leaps but reinforcing and expanding existing skills. I was reassured by her inextinguishable smile, but some days Mrs. Gardner must have felt like a cheerleader in a gym full of somnambulists.

We read alone more often that year, but periodically met in small groups to perform for Mrs. Gardner. I remember our primer's male protagonist, Robert. Many of the stories revolved around Robert's friendship with a hobo named Zeke. Zeke, who may or may not have had substance abuse problems, found employment as a handyman when absolutely necessary. Though plainly rootless, the neighborhood didn't mind his presence or frequent interaction with their children. To youngsters, Zeke was the only adult who always had time to listen.

Typical plots featured children becoming self-sufficient citizens under Zeke's subversive tutelage. For example, when Robert expressed his desire for bigger arm muscles, Zeke might have designed a weight resistance program with isometric components for the boy. Instead, he pulled one of those Tom Sawyer-white-washing-the-fence scams. "Robert, I'll need to sleep on that problem," said Zeke. Since the hobo recently made a deal to turn a fallen tree into firewood, Robert volunteered to chop wood until a solution revealed itself in Zeke's dreams. Predictably, the process took longer than expected but, by the time Robert balked, the daily workouts had produced results. Everybody won. Robert got muscles and learned the nobility of physical labor. Zeke got paid to sleep.

The primer's moralistic tone found expression in almost everything we did that year. For instance, although we had been banking thorough a community sponsored program since kindergarten, this year whole lessons were devoted to the virtues of saving. Example math problems illustrated how weekly deposits of pennies compounded at 1.5% could multiply into tens of dollars during our seven-year tenure at SoCal Elementary.

We always participated in Junior Fire Marshalls. In the past, students were given plastic fire hats and badges for returning a fire safety brochure, one the family supposedly reviewed together but more likely was signed on the run that very morning. During 3rd grade, the incentive ante was upped to include wearing real fire-fighting equipment and riding a fire truck. In return, children inspected their homes, room by room, and reported any safety violations they discovered. When parents signed their child's inspection sheet, the implicit agreement was to correct all violations in a timely manner. I can't confirm promises were kept but, like much of 50s suburbia, the activity had a Big Brother ambiance.

That year, even art sessions degenerated into experiments of social engineering. Art for art's sake was replaced with a utilitarian aesthetic. No longer could we paint or sculpt what was in our hearts, instead our skill with tempera and Play-

Doh was harnessed for a greater, communal good. From a pragmatic view, Mrs. Gardner's grocery store project was genius. Building and operating the classroom store would provide teachable moments in math, history, and economics while honing the students' communicative and social skills. Probably, it did all those things but at the price of my soul. I loved art just a little less than reading. By third grade, I was already a confirmed paint and brush guy, so this project made no use of my best talent.

Against the entire length of one wall, Mrs. Gardner's husband built a counter, vegetable bins, and shelves for cans. She sewed a red and white awning and supplied a cash register with fake money. Everyone brought canned goods to stock the shelves but we had to make replica meat, fruit and vegetables since real ones would rot. Mrs. Gardner also provided a garbage can filled with papier-mâché. Her plan was to organize teams to produce an inventory with the optimum ratio of foodstuffs.

My classmates acted enthused about crafting facsimile asparagus, cauliflower, pineapples, pork chops, and so on. I couldn't get as excited since I was assigned to the potato team. How much skill is required to produce a papier-mâché potato? Make a fist; make a potato. Painting the dried lumps was equally challenging - brown. The potato team reached their quota so quickly that Mrs. Gardner bought time by requiring black dots for eyes. She was a very nice woman but sometimes third grade was oppressive.

Can't Always Get What You Want

Rather than a typical arrangement like two lines of classrooms under a single roof sharing a common hallway, our elementary classrooms were modular. The school was constructed from pods of six classrooms each, three on either side of a common wall, with doors opening to the outside. These parallel annexes were connected by covered sidewalks and concrete stairs. In the past, whole grade levels were confined to single pods, but recent enrollment forced abandonment of that organization. That's why I could see Mr. Gabriel' sixth grade classroom in the adjacent wing from my fourth grade window.

I wished I was old enough to be in his class, but Miss Riley was my fourth grade teacher. It was common for principals to be men but Mr. Gabriel was the only male teacher in elementary school. I heard he taught slower kids than we had in our class. However, if given a choice between quality education and having him for my teacher, I wouldn't have thought twice. Miss Riley meant well but she was useless at impromptu games of flag football.

Mr. Gabriel was slender and had closely cropped hair. He usually wore sports coats or trim suits that made him look like TV's Dick Van Dyke. If he wore a sweater, he wore a tie as well. Whatever Mr. Gabriel' actual age, confidence made him seem young. His clipped speech and quick movements lent intensity absent in other adults. His manner suggested he was forever holding something in check, like a coiled spring. He could end playground scuffles with a word or just his disapproving scowl. Minutes later he'd have the same hooligans laughing and shaking hands. My friends all wished we had a place in his circle.

I respected Miss Riley, too, but for different things. She was the first teacher to let us decorate the classroom. When we studied California history, she covered the back bulletin board with a swath of white butcher paper. Then she had Terrence and me design a mural for the whole class to color. She insisted any design we chose was okay as long as it reflected our reading. To reach our target blood and gore quota, we bent the parameters of time and geography to incorporate buffalo hunts, Little Bighorn, and Aztec human sacrifices but Miss Riley didn't complain.

She also organized field trips to places outside the city like a dairy to see electric milking machines and a gourd farm where an old man turned dried gourds into bowls and birdhouses. After the dairy trip we shook cream-filled mason jars to make butter we spread on saltines. A few days before winter vacation, Miss Riley brought spools of cotton wick, jars of silver glitter, and red sheets of bees wax so we could make candles as Christmas gifts. She was also a supporter of the school's hobby and flower show.

Once a year, PTA women visited the classroom to judge our collections and skills at flower arranging. To ensure the work was ours, we completed flower arrangements in the presence of stopwatch-holding judges. It wasn't cheating exactly, but I practiced my arrangement at home several times before the contest. Mom, who once worked for a florist, came up with the design I used to snag a blue ribbon that year and for several years after.

My winning arrangement required a shallow, rectangular vase, a metal frog secured with florist's clay, and three flower varieties from our garden. When completed, four huge balls of white hydrangeas rested on a purple layer of straw flowers. Three bird of paradise stocks of varying length thrust upward through the hydrangea blossoms, their orange and purple blooms in dramatic contrast with a fan-like backdrop of dark, green ferns. It was simple and elegant. The shell collection that won a red ribbon in hobbies was all my doing.

Sputnik

I was seven when Sputnik was launched which suggests I shouldn't remember much. But I do. America promised the world a weather satellite in 1959 to celebrate the Geophysical Year, but then Sputnik shattered complacency like another Pearl Harbor and the world was hi-jacked by heathens.

That October I sat on the living room couch with an open newspaper. Flanked by my parents and sister, the four of us studied illustrations of a sky divided into sectors. Even as we struggled with new vocabulary to explain what was happening, saying *Sputnik* aloud left a bad aftertaste.

For the next several nights, my family huddled on our front lawn and searched the sky. Neighbors living on either side did the same, all of us using copies of the same newsprint star map. Occasionally, someone shouted "There!" but most likely he was mistaken. In the beginning, people were easily fooled by airplane lights and shooting stars. Before we became comfortable with one Russian satellite overhead, they orbited another.

Sputnik II was launched a month after the first. The novelty was this time the spacecraft carried a passenger - a dog named Laika. Americans got to know her from a grainy, B&W clip that ran endlessly on TV. Tongue hanging, tail wagging, Laika was strapped to the capsule's floor with a leather harness. She wore the expression of imploring friendliness that domestic animals get when they're scared. All I could think was *how lonely*. It turned out the Russians never had any intention of bringing her home. Provisions for the dog's return were never made or even considered. That is the kind of people we were dealing with.

Later, on my walking route to the beach, there was a hobby store that featured a window display with Liaka's satellite. The Revell model featured long, sweeping antennae attached to a globe of molded plates and simulated rivets. Unlike the real Sputnik, this sphere's top half was clear plastic so the replica dog inside could be seen. Even though she was no longer in the news, Laika's image still made me sad. I couldn't look at her without wondering when she gave up, when she understood they weren't coming back for her. Whether Laika starved or suffocated before burning up during re-entry six months later, the TV never said.

After a year of humiliating and very public failures, the United States finally orbited an Explorer satellite. Of course, by then the Russians controlled space. Everybody knew that because the daily papers featured front-page charts, like baseball box scores, comparing the number and tonnage of space probes by both nations. The coverage and tone of the news was changing in less obvious ways as well. *Russians* became *Reds* and increasingly headlines featured phrases like *Krushchev Demands, Krushchev Threatens.*

At some point, most Americans grasped the space race was not just about satellites. It was about *them* and *us.* Then my family held a new meeting on the living room couch. This time Dad described an underground shelter he could build using blueprints published in *Life* magazine. He said afterwards we'd vote whether the family savings would be spent for a backyard swimming pool or a fallout shelter. In the end, we got neither.

Maybe Americans tolerated uncertainty better in those days, but I don't remember people voicing every question inside their heads. I don't remember people going berserk and hurting strangers because they were frustrated by the way things were. We thought about the greater good in those days. That was the case during duck and cover drills at school. When the siren sounded, we climbed beneath our desks as instructed. With hands clasped behind neck, chin to chest, and knees pulled up, we made ourselves as small as possible. We shrank like flowers in reverse - bloom to bud. When our teacher said the brown vinyl curtains would save us from flying glass, no one asked why glass would be breaking. We cooperated and listened for the all-clear.

Space Race

The first clipping in my scrapbook described the Russians hitting the moon with a rocket in 1959, but it was the Mercury Seven who held my attention as a child. Each of the first six astronauts - Shepard, Grissom, Glenn, Carpenter, Schirra, and Cooper (Slayton didn't go) - got front page coverage, magazine covers, and parades. I saved their stories in a scrapbook Mom and I made from wide rolls of brown wrapping paper. The pages were hand cut and held together with a stapled edge because the clippings were too large to fit a regular book.

Every blastoff was televised from Cape Canaveral, Florida. Because of time zones, on launch days I had to wake as early as 5 AM in California. My folks never joined me, but they didn't mind if the sound was kept low enough for them to sleep. I held many pre-dawn vigils with a bowl of sugared Jets, staring at the Indian head test pattern, hoping the mission wouldn't be scrubbed. If things went smoothly (which was rare - *t-minus 2 hours, 20 minutes, and holding*), I still could make school by 8. Without VCRs or Tivos, history had to be witnessed live.

It's hard to believe we used to care so much. Today's technologically jaded citizens probably consider those early forays into space to be quaint. I've heard it claimed the Apollo moon craft featured less technology than today's average home computer or even some multifunction phones. If that's true, rather than disparage early space exploration, we should marvel at how much was accomplished with so little. Like Columbus did with those three secondhand ships. Traveling to the moon (even to hit golf balls) surely is better use of science than forwarding jokes at the speed of light or twittering about an awesome salad.

As a kid I lay in tall, summer grass and searched for faces and animals in the clouds. Whenever my family camped, locating the North Star and the Big Dipper was a nighttime game. Even before Sputnik, we studied the sky. The foreboding, however, was new. For us, that began with government reassurances Russian satellites weren't big enough to carry bombs. After Sputnik, we still knew where heaven was but it seemed less exclusive.

Nixon's The One

I developed an early appreciation for sarcasm from my mother and her two sisters. Together, their humor was as dry as fall leaves. It was rare for both aunts to visit us at the same time, so their chat sessions are epic in my memory. When they shared a room, the present didn't exist. Three grown women instantly reverted to the pecking order of their youth; conjuring dark and hilariously human tales still fixed in undead sibling rivalry. The best place to witness group therapy was in silence at my mother's feet.

Truth was triangulated during those sessions. My aunts used dining chairs dragged to the living room. They sat near each other; back straight, knees together, and folded hands on lap. All spoke in the same conspiratorial monotone, never stepped on another's punch line, and delivered streams of lacerating commentary through barely parted, whispering lips with hardly an audible chuckle. Mrs. Sullivan, my 5th grade teacher, could have been the fourth sister, separated at birth.

Mrs. Sullivan was old and cranky but certainly not mean. However, as a teacher she was a shock after years of younger, nurturing types. Fifth grade under Mrs. Sullivan's direction held no surprises. As we grinded through the lessons, it was obvious she was mentally checking boxes on a list perfected eons earlier. That's not to say her methods weren't efficient; they simply weren't inspiring, not even to her anymore. It's a poor magician who can't feign enthusiasm for her own tricks.

Mrs. Sullivan's ways lulled us more than bored us. As children on the cusp of adolescence, we discovered comfort in education that lacked immediacy. In fact, no one enjoyed temporary reprieve from the daily script more than our teacher.

Technology was rare in those days so it was shared. Mrs.

Sullivan showed many 16-millimeter movies that year. The films rarely had any obvious relevance to what we were studying, but that never mattered. On Wednesdays, usually an hour after lunch, class was interrupted by timid knocking. Typically, Mrs. Sullivan made a show of slamming shut her textbook and huffed indignation as she retrieved the projector cart parked outside the classroom door.

"These aren't the films I ordered!" she invariably exclaimed. After more muttering to establish disgust and frustration, she'd say something to the class like, "We've been talking about the Industrial Revolution but it might be interesting to know more about Indian sand painting and how to improve our table manners. Children, what do you think?" We never objected. The class and Mrs. Sullivan had an understanding. Besides, ignoring the curriculum occasionally led to some really interesting stuff.

Mrs. Sullivan didn't hate children, but she'd been in the education business long enough to lose common illusions about them. She wasn't what is now called "child-centered." Interactions with her students weren't designed to encourage reflection or critical thinking but to get their mind right. If an opinion was called for, Mrs. Sullivan gave us one. For me, not thinking was a real timesaver but occasionally proved troublesome. Like during the 1960 World Series.

Mrs. Sullivan was a huge baseball fan. I have to give her that. Since more baseball was played during daytime than under lights in those days, following the World Series was nearly impossible for a school kid, even one with plenty of bathroom passes and a hidden transistor radio. For this series, however, Mrs. Sullivan brought her TV from home. Not purely for the love of the game, mind you, but because she was a Yankee fan. Naturally, my classmates (who didn't know baseball anyway) also became ardent New York fans for a week. That left just a couple of us guys to root for Pittsburgh.

The series went 7 games with the Yankees outhitting and outscoring the Pirates but losing when Bill Mazeroski became the first player to hit a walk-off home run to win a World Series. We ached to scream, "Told you so!" but hid our joy because Teacher was such a bad loser.

A month later, we clashed over the presidential election. Predictably, Mrs, Sullivan, the Yankee lover, was also an unrepentant Kennedy supporter. *He's so handsome!* Like most 10 year-olds, I endorsed the politics of my parents, which made me a Nixon man. When JFK was inaugurated, she brought her TV again for the swearing in. I wanted to be civil but for god's sake the man couldn't even pronounce *America* properly. Plus, what about when the Pope started calling shots in the White House? "What about then?" I wanted to ask her. Of course, that conversation never happened because Mrs. Sullivan was also an ungracious winner.

Still, I have some nice memories of that year. All classrooms in the fifth grade wing had flagstone patios attached. Outdoors on spring afternoons, using a portable record player whose electrical cord snaked through an open window, we were taught to dance. In those days, square dancing seemed a reasonable way to introduce social graces and provide early forays into boy-girl relations. Our class practiced every other Friday.

It was against the rules to always dance with the same person, but my favorite partner was Sylvia who was chubby in good way. She had a wonderful smile and freckles across her nose. Sylvia's shiny hair bounced whenever she moved and I liked the feel of my arm around her thick waist. Our families went to the same Methodist church, which meant we also attended the same youth activities outside of school. Once at a church-sponsored square dance, several adults remarked how well we looked together.

Mrs. Sullivan's dreaded end-of-the-year activity was called Partner Projects: two classmates planned and executed a learning display and were awarded a single grade for their joint effort. Whether it was Mrs. Sullivan's nod to cooperative learning or merely a clever way to cut her grading in half, Partner Projects was serious stuff.

To ensure graduation from fifth grade, Eddie and I decided to construct a relief map of the recently admitted states, Alaska and Hawaii. Dad cut a piece of plywood big enough for the display, about 18 inches square. Mom supervised mixing sculpting dough from flour, water, and paste that would stick to the plywood. Eddie's sole contribution was buying two small American flags, one with 49 stars and the other with 50, to dress up our display on project day.

I did the sculpting, painting, and lettering that identified major cities and significant geographic features. I didn't mind because it proved fun and I was certain we'd earn high marks. On judgment day, Eddie and I stood at attention while the unsmiling, note-scribbling Mrs. Sullivan critiqued of our work. After a few minutes, without even acknowledging our presence, she was ready to move on.

When it became clear she wasn't going to end the suspense, I blurted at her back, "What about the grade?" The way Mrs. Sullivan spun, lowered her clipboard, and glared, suggested my actions were as impertinent as Tiny Tim demanding another bowl of gruel.

While leisurely adjusting her glasses, Mrs. Sullivan

offered that I'd been inconsistent with scale while molding my doughy landscape. Mount McKinley was indeed the highest point in North America, she conceded, but it should not be five inches tall on this relief map. She also snidely opined it was doubtful that Juneau residents could see the Hawaiian Islands from their kitchen windows. (Obviously she was right, but squeezing two states onto the same small board required artistic license.) Finally, she criticized the number of mountains decorated with streams of red paint in my version of Hawaii. Her point was that not every hill in Hawaii is an active volcano. I understood the objection but believed Mrs. Sullivan was shortsighted for discounting the drama lava flows added to our presentation.

As for our project grade, Mrs. Sullivan left us twisting in the wind for another week. In the end, my subjective vision of America's newest states earned *C*'s for Eddie and me. That was good news but even better was my nomination to the Safety Patrol. Since Mr. Gabriel didn't know me from Adam, it had to be a teacher's recommendation that did it. Sixth grade was looking a whole lot better, thanks to good, old Mrs. Sullivan.

Dixie

She was naturally giant and crane-like, but Mrs. Nelson loved wearing high heels with straight skirts and frilly blouses. Her teased, bleached hair had the spun quality of cotton candy styled into a permanently lacquered bubble. She spent a lot of time getting pretty. Up close, her face was all powder and rouge with details penciled in, blue eyelids and red lipstick that made her mouth even bigger. Mrs. Nelson's southern drawl was the first I'd heard outside of TV and movies. Fifteen minutes into our first meeting, the class was mimicking her accent as she led us in song: *I stuck my head in a little skunk's hole.* That was pretty hilarious the first few times. "Cielito Lindo" was another tune she never tired of. *Ay, ay, ay, ay*. The die was cast.

As the final year of elementary school, I expected sixth grade to be my best. It wasn't completely disastrous but it was the first time my charm and natural strengths carried no weight with a teacher. I certainly didn't enjoy singing, not even about skunks. Mrs. Nelson assigned a lot of reading (I was a good reader) but chose stories featuring lost animals that eventually found their way home after much adversity. And she didn't appreciate non-fiction at all. On my own, I had already read everything about Balboa, Cortez, and DeSoto. The city library branch near my house had an entire shelf dedicated to Spanish explorers. Each matching volume featured a gray cloth cover with the explorer's name stamped in silver on a red binding. My goal was to read all 20.

You'd think anyone who liked Spanish songs so much would find it interesting that the name of the guy who explored Florida in 1528 means *head of a cow.* That's right. Alvar Nunez *Cabesa de Vaca.* Alvar Nunez *Head of a Cow.* I offered that fun fact while the class was learning lyrics for "La Cucaracha." Mrs. Nelson stared like I was from Mars and, without comment, resumed her lesson. Since the 4th grade, my drawing skills earned me a spot on every class mural or decorating project. Predictably, a teacher who didn't value Spanish explorers wouldn't appreciate my talent for replicating bloody historical scenes and I couldn't sketch a decent deer or squirrel to save my life. If battling Incas and Aztec human sacrifices were out, then so was I.

As it happened, I shouldn't have fretted because Mrs. Nelson never decorated the room with student work anyway. I guess that's something better suited for younger grades. Instead, she changed the bulletin boards herself every month to reflect the season and upcoming holidays.

My teacher had personality and endless enthusiasm, but school didn't fit very well during sixth grade. My restlessness wasn't her fault. Since the previous summer's family vacation, my parents dropped hints we might sell our house and move to Arizona. Such a move struck me as very unlikely since it meant leaving my grandparents, the cousins, and everyone but it weighed on me nonetheless. More likely I was getting worked up about next fall and 7th grade. Junior high still was months away but I've always over-thought change to the point of paralysis.

Everyday we took breaks from math and science instruction to sing or listen while Teacher pounded out some corny tune on her blond upright piano. She also introduced us to *good* music. I never decided whether Mrs. Nelson had unusually strong convictions about music education or sometimes just needed a break from being bubbly, but a weekly ration of classical music was courtesy of her and the Standard Oil Company of California.

During one of their radio broadcasts on a particularly warm afternoon, when every head rested on a desktop and we all fought sleep, I first heard *Rhapsody in Blue.* The class radio that was delivered on a rolling cart sometimes was replaced by a record player. Part of Mrs. Nelson's culture arsenal was the complete "Victory at Sea" soundtrack on vinyl discs. We fought a lot of sea battles that spring.

Sixth grade wasn't terrible. My grades were okay but sometimes I felt banished to a world meant for girls. Thankfully, the Safety Patrol gave me an excuse to meet with the guys and Mr. Gabriel almost every day.

Friday's Child

Pouty Claire had a heart-shaped face and immense green eyes. Plastic berets pulled the loose, blond curls away from her face; a style that exaggerated her eyes and diminished her chin. Petticoats, short velvet jackets, and sometimes gloves or the unnecessary purse made Claire's wardrobe more appropriate for church than school. During sixth grade, her favorite accessory was a strip of white rabbit fur shaped into a child's fox stole. Detailed with glass eyes, leather paws, and a tail, the boys joked her fashionable stole actually was an animal someone ran over. What appeared to be the flattened fox's teeth were the serrated jaws of a metal spring-loaded clip. By making the animal bite its own tail, Claire kept the fur positioned around her shoulders. That fox stole proved both emblematic of Claire's persona and instrumental in our breakup.

Breakup suggests sophistication not in play during elementary days. I had several girlfriends before Claire, ones of my choosing. Probably, few were aware they'd been designated my girl friend because love was a tacit emotion then. Girlfriends smiled back from across a room. Girlfriends giggled with their friends when you walked by. A girlfriend was the one who made your face flush when you said her name aloud. Love began as implicit understanding and required no expression more bold than exchanged Valentines.

I loved Leisha, who had the darkest skin in kindergarten. I loved Abby in 3rd grade for reasons no more complicated than we both liked to draw. And, of course, there was Sheila, my 5th grade dance partner. I'm certain Shelia grew into one of those iconic American beauties, but I loved her when she could have passed for one of Dick and Jane's sunny, water-colored neighbor. So Claire wasn't my first girlfriend but she was the first to sour love with betrayal - making it more grownup.

By sixth grade, boys had no say in matters of schoolyard romance. Couples regularly were created and dissolved by votes among councils of girls. Late that spring I was informed by two girls (both unknown to me) that Claire thought I was cute and I was her boyfriend. The news didn't make me overly anxious. In my experience, being a boyfriend carried no special responsibilities. Boys were completely out of the loop and basically did whatever they did normally and waited for further instructions.

In the case of Claire and me, we were over before we began. Our falling out happened on the playground. I was battling a foursquare opponent as Claire stood behind me, cheering, as she should. Classmates yelped delight each time I slammed my foe. Their encouragement gave me incredible focus and enough savagery to win. Only when I stooped to retrieve the game ball did I understand they were hooting at me.

In the heat of battle, Claire playfully clipped her fox stole to the bottom hem of my shirt. The cheers I heard were actually laughter at my *tail.* I grabbed the flat, dead fox, threw it to the ground, and glared at Claire. We still weren't talking the next day. Next recess, I didn't let her win like boyfriends do. I beat her at every game and humiliated her in front of our schoolmates. She cried when I took aim at her over everyone else in the dodge ball ring. After that, no one had to tell me that Claire and I were through.

Love is patient, love is kind. It does not envy, it does not boast. And love doesn't make a boyfriend the butt of jokes.

CHAPTER 10

Our Most Important Product

I Spy

Our first granddaughter was a toddler when we followed her folks from city to country and built a house near theirs. Since everyone worked different hours in town, Grandma and Pop-Pop often were taxi service from babysitter to home. When my wife and I were children, we rode the front seats of huge, steel vehicles whose only seatbelts were the driver's right arm. Today, laws banish the youngest to rear seats and even require some carriers to face backward. I'd expect babies to get lonely but maybe everyone craves quiet moments. Besides, whether it was another juice box or endless replays of her favorite song on the car's tape deck, the grandchild in the backseat made her wants known.

I'd grown tired of the town where I worked, but sometimes the natural beauty at its outskirts lifted my gloom. Traveling with the baby helped even more. Once we were lost in separate worlds while driving home. It was one of those sunny, winter mornings when country sky is infinite, cloudless, and Kodachrome blue like skies in old vacation slides. Suddenly, the voice from the backseat insisted we look, look now. "It's scratching the sky!" she cried. Since I wasn't driving, I slid lower to see what the baby saw. It was only an airplane leaving a vapor trail, but for some reason she saw a tool like a box knife scraping the painted surface of a vast glass pane, scratching away enough blue paint to reveal the gleaming undercoating of white.

It's easy to forget Nature's fundamental elegance when power lines or careless architecture obscures it. Worry and prejudice make me just as myopic. Sometimes, chancing a new route is enough to derail complacency. Other times, it takes new eyes; ones not yet dulled to wonder.

Machines And Men

If our neighborhood served in polite defense of sweet normalcy, then Dad's backyard shop threatened it all. His building hammered, buzzed, smoked, and shook all the live-long day. The ceiling's flickering banks of florescent tubes allowed Dad's men to work late into the night. With electric saws, routers, and claw hammer percussion, they produced a mad, discordant symphony. My father conducted daily.

The choreography was wondrous. A stream of custom cabinetry, doors, and Formica countertops shot through an overhead door in back - all loaded into trucks headed for The Job. The building behind our house reeked with foreign smells; exotic combinations of paint, sawdust, adhesives, and overheated electric motors.

Mom said the shop was crammed with junk, but there was masculine priority to the chaos. He had wall bins for lumber, drawers for nails and seldom used tools, designated areas for woodworking and another for metal. I grew up knowing my Dad could build anything. The junk in that shop was clay he molded and gave life. When I was small and he was working, I never clung to his pants leg for he was pure motion. The best I could do was playing in tandem with the slower workers.

My favorite corner was taken by an oil-drenched, L-shape of waist high benches. Those thick wooden tabletops held a metal lathe, a grinder, and a bolted-down, blue iron vise. On the walls were racks that held jars of drill bits, wood screws, and hinges. The counter was layered with hand tools like wire strippers, tin snips, files, and pliers. I was happy when someone scarred a wood chisel because then Dad used the grinder.

A metal shaft ran through the center of the green, encased electric motor. On one end of the shaft was a stiff wire brush for cleaning rust. On the other end was a grinding wheel. The damaged chisel shrieked when it touched the spinning stone. A fountain of yellow sparks flowed from the chisel's edge, hit my father's chest and turned orange, then blue, before dying on his boots. It was like he was being swarmed by fireflies and I marveled that he never burst into flames.

Sometimes I'd disappear into the metal corner and run my fingers through the shavings' rough gray curls. Standing on a box and flipping dead electrical switches, I pretended I was commanding a submarine. The lathe's cutting head could be positioned by hand-turning a series of small chrome wheels. With each revolution, the cutter slid farther along narrow tracks lined with long strips of silver ball bearings that resembled the studded hatbands worn by stylish TV cowboys. Other times, to feel as strong as Superman, I used the vise to crush pop cans or splinter scraps of wood. In the metal corner I was out of the way but saw everything.

In my father's shop I never built anything. No matter how I tried, I didn't have the gift. From the time I was very small, we made different use of the same tools. It's taken two lifetimes to accommodate that.

D.I.Y.

Some boomers perpetuate the impression they were so deprived as children their only toys were potatoes, mud, and sharp sticks. That certainly wasn't the case in my working class neighborhood. There were toys for sale without the variety common today. The toy industry wasn't yet sophisticated enough to niche market or assault consumers with coordinated sales campaigns involving TV, movies, and fast food franchises. (In fact, I was 10 by the time big burger chains came into their own.) My closet shelves held sports equipment, art supplies, board games, and shoeboxes of yo-yos, gyroscopes, tops, metal cars, plastic army men, magnifying glasses, marbles, and stacks of bubblegum cards organized with rubber bands; not that much different from children today.

Although the quantity and quality aren't comparable, most of us had enough store-bought playthings. The difference is we also made toys. The real treasure on my closet shelves was stuff Mom kept trying to throw away – the empty coffee cans and egg cartons, balls of string, odd lengths of wire, metal washers scavenged from building sites, cigar boxes, bundles of Popsicle sticks, the iron from my old wood burning kit with the electrical short. Scout manuals or magazines like *Boys' Life* and *Junior Highlights* regularly featured kids' do-it-yourself projects. Once my dad demonstrated how to make a *car* from an empty thread spool, toothpick, rubber band, and sliver of soap, if you can imagine a *car* with no fenders and only two wheels. (My young son wasn't impressed either when I sprang it on him thirty years later. That time, the hardest part was locating a wooden spool.)

The best project from my father's olden days was crystal radio sets. Stripping insulation from copper wire and wrapping it around a cardboard tube was time-consuming but not impossible for stubby little fingers. It was also an opportunity to learn soldering basics. True, our radio didn't have an amplified speaker and stations were locked using an alligator clip, but snatching music from the sky without batteries or electricity was a miracle. Dad placed the works into a backless pine and Masonite box he attached to the side rail of my bunk bed. In place of the absent speaker was a hardwired pair of old Navy headphones that were black metal and made even heavier by the massive magnets inside them. Just their weight gave me headaches, but I loved falling asleep with talk and music inside my head.

To make toys, it wasn't always necessary (or advisable) to

get adult help. For instance, any kid who wanted a skateboard had one because ours weren't finely engineered fiberglass creations; they literally were wooden boards with skate wheels attached. Kids' metal skates clamped to the soles of their street shoes. Sliding front and rear plates with steel wheels made the skate adjustable to shoe length. Because they were so durable, it wasn't difficult to locate a forgotten, hand-me-down skate somewhere to cannibalize.

After removing the bolt connecting the sliding halves, we nailed a wheeled plate to either end of a short pine board. I preferred a length of 2X4 scrap from Dad's shop and several industrial strength 16p nails. About the time I lost interest in skateboards, the local bike shop started selling rubber wheels with ball bearings to replace the metal ones purloined from our sisters' skates. We had no way of imagining what technology would offer skateboarding kids of the future.

The junk on my closet shelves rarely became components in thoughtfully executed projects. Most often, our imaginations ran miles ahead of our manual skills. Still, I'm glad we had the opportunity to assemble disparate parts intuitively and misuse tools. Without adult tunnel vision guiding our every effort, free-range kids were more likely to investigate than label. Exploration doesn't need to be profound to be valuable.

For instance, with adult supervision a magnifying glass from the dime stone could have introduced us to nature's fractals, but on our own we learned to burn holes in newspaper and incinerate ants. Since long ago only wealthy people golfed, we had no opportunity to use a found golf ball properly. Instead, girls who played jacks coveted one because of the ball's hang time. Boys used them for handball because of their liveliness against a stucco wall. Since many of our golf balls had been discarded with a cover gash, they didn't always serve those alternative purposes. However, if today's children were trusted with pocketknives like we were, they'd know even a damaged golf ball has entertainment potential.

Directions: Remove the remaining cover with a knife to expose the ball of rubber bands within. Slash the top layer with your blade and drop the ball to the ground. As the unraveling strands release pressure, the ball jumps and bounces of its own accord while dragging the ever-lengthening strings. When decompression is complete, the resulting rubber spaghetti pile will be 20 times the volume of the original ball. The process is livelier and longer lasting than the average can of silly-string plus it's free. However, buried deep within the golf ball remnants is a marble-sized rubber core. Exercise caution when handling the core. Discard it immediately. I never tried myself, but there were stories about a kid who cut into a golf ball core. Turned out it had a liquid center that squirted into his eyes and blinded him for life. I'm just sayin'.

Men, A Baby, And Machines

Brother Frank was always more contented among Dad's men and machines than I was. As a preschooler, he spent full days in the backyard shop. Dad's small crew were usually pretty good people and unusually tolerant of the boss's kids. They made room for Frank and supplied him with lumber scraps and all the sawdust he wanted.

One workman in particular was an idol of Frank's. His name was Max Hinkle. If not for Max, my brother would be a vegetarian today. As far as the family knew, prior to a cookout at the Hinkle's, red meat had never passed Frank's lips. Until age four or five, his idea of a great hamburger was toasted buns with mustard but no beef.

Max, who was a few years younger than my Dad, was gangly with unruly black hair. I don't know if he could be called handsome, but his good humor and easygoing ways made him fun for kids to be around. Max had boys of his own but seemed genuinely fond of our Babe and amused by his talent for mimicry. For his part, Frank was convinced that everything the man said was true. It was Max who taught

Frank to spit on each piece of wood before nailing them together. Apparently spit acts as a kind of glue that positions the boards until the first nail is started. Babe shared this building tip with Dad but never convinced him.

Max was a jokester but sometimes even misinformation is better than no guidance. A kid misses certain nuances when he learns only through observation. For instance, when Dad faced a repetitive hammering task, he held a few spare nails between his lips, like a cigarette, to save the wasted motion of reaching again into his nail apron. Untutored, Frank's flawed version of that technique was tossing a handful of eight penny nails into his mouth all at once like M&Ms.

Frank quickly became a fixture and the stealthy toddler moved through the shop like a ninja, apparently invisible to Dad and his men. The more he exercised his imagination, the more frequent and bold his mischief became. Once, Frank grew weary of painting with the brush and water supplied to him. He decided he needed paint from the wall shelves for his latest project. As a toddler, he could reach the paint shelf only by standing atop one of the workbenches. He could pull himself atop the workbench only by climbing a lumber stack. He could only climb the lumber stack by first building it from floor scraps around the feet of the shop's busy crew. Standing on top of the bench, straining on tiptoes and reaching over his head, Frank finally grabbed the desired paint can which fell on him.

Mom was not forgiving when she returned home from the church potluck and found her youngest covered head to toe with pink enamel. I remember how Brother sat calmly in the bathtub with his puffy red eyes and *What? Me worry?* grin as my father furiously scrubbed Frank's little body with a turpentine rag and sputtered incomprehension concerning how such a thing could have happened.

Boxes

They could have been pigmy tribesmen returning from a hunt, breaking through the mist with an antelope carcass held high above their heads, but it was just Jerry and his buddies carrying a refrigerator box. Most Southern Californian landscapes don't resemble the vaporous crags of Skull Island, but beach towns can look downright primordial before the mid-morning sun burns off the fog. This morning, the mist only added drama to the gang's triumphant return.

During the summer, we held box stakeouts behind the appliance store. Not that we were the only ones; we competed against scouts from other neighborhoods as well. Commonly, stores shredded boxes to pack trash tighter, but sometimes employees just undid the end flaps and collapsed them. If flattened that way, a box could be restored with masking tape. The ideal scenario was to intercept stock boys who'd rather have us haul away the boxes than deal with their disposal. Today, diligence, good fortune, and employee laziness led to our capture of the Kenmore beast.

The worth of an intact refrigerator box during my childhood can't be overstated. Hypothetically, an antelope might feed a village for a day but a large cardboard box provided my neighborhood with a week of entertainment. Historians marvel how little waste was tolerated when Plains Indians butchered a buffalo, but we put the same effort into rendering a refrigerator box. Not only was it the largest box made, the cardboard's thicker gauge and capped ends held with metal bands made it the sturdiest. On its side, that big box might be a bus, tank, or submarine. Vertically, it was a rocket ship, jail, or stagecoach.

Although a refrigerator box was the Grail, we scrambled for anything big enough to crawl into. My sister, brother, and I once made a computer from an oversized box. We painted over the outside printing and renamed it Univac. Two people inside were required to make it work. On the outside were mail slots (one for questions and another for answers), fake dials, and a series of jets made from sections of soda straws.

When a third party fed a written question into the machine, a flashlight (whose lens poked though the cardboard) was lit to indicate the computer was thinking. From inside, one worker composed a written answer while the other twirled the ends of toothpicks attached to needles on the outside dials and gauges. Sound effects for the thinking computer were produced by beating saucepans with a tinker toy. Finally, in the climatic moments before the machine spit its response from the answer slot, dramatic blasts of smoke (Mom's scented talcum powder) shot from the straw jets.

Not every box's fate was so elaborate, but all were repurposed. My sister used smaller boxes for Barbie dollhouses. Other girls decorated cigar boxes with fabric and white glue to hold treasures. With plastic figurines, sand, gravel, and construction paper, shoeboxes were routinely transformed into dioramas depicting war scenes or battling dinosaurs. Once I rescued enough cardboard from the kitchen trash to build a large, scaled city in my backyard, only to destroy it as Godzilla would. Another memorable time, I used a box to nearly kill my sister.

In the presence of my aged mother, I still affect repentance and horror at my recklessness that day long ago. However, since it wasn't premeditated cruelty and at 50 my sister displays only minor traces of scarring, I still smile at the memory while acknowledging that's shameful, too. Although a perfectly delightful adult now, once Diana was a pesky seven-year-old determined to tag along with the McCarthy boys and me.

To keep her home, we devised a scheme involving a tall, narrow box that once held shelving my father ordered. After breaking out both ends of the empty box, we slipped it over my standing sister like a big sock. Fortuitously, the box dimensions matched hers. With only her head and feet sticking out, she looked like an upright book or a branchless tree in a bad school play. Without arms to swing, hands to grab, or knees to bend, we figured she'd be immobilized long enough for us to escape. Our plan would have worked handily if only Diana hadn't been so foolishly determined to follow.

I turned in time to see her fall like a cardboard obelisk in slow motion. The terror in her little face when she realized she couldn't cushion the fall is fixed in my memory. The saucer-sized eyes and the endless *Ohooooo* escaping her mouth were pure Tom and Jerry. After she met the concrete, I fully expected Diana would shake her head and the dents would pop out with cartoon efficiency. I was very wrong. Stitches were required and I should have been beaten severely.

From my experience as a grandfather, I attest time and technology hasn't dampened children's natural affinity for cardboard. An empty box is still an embodiment of possibility. When rough play flattened a refrigerator box, we removed the ends and rolled down grass hills four at a time, side-by-side in the wide paper band. And when that cardboard loop snapped, we fashioned individual sleds and took the hill again. With a new box, I delayed the first cut as long as possible to avoid mistakes. Although anxiety never kept the box from evolving, today clean canvases and empty computer screens evoke the same insecurity and evasion.

Ski-Daddle

Forgotten against one shop wall was the abandoned wood skeleton of an unfinished ski boat. The rough keel and ribs lay like the remains of a filleted whale. It stayed untouched for most of my early childhood. There were many false starts.

Once, Dad bought another boat for salvage. It was a cartoonish craft; a daydream refined too many times, executed by someone with too many boating magazines and too little skill. It was poorly proportioned with a towering cabin perched atop a severe, crescent hull painted red, white, and blue. My parents argued over the $175 it cost. He insisted it would produce an engine, shaft and propeller, a steering mechanism, deck hardware, and a trailer. After a week spent stripping the boat to a pile of rotting wood and taking three loads to the dump, the only usable thing the battered hulk gave us was a brass bell with a leather thong tied to the clacker.

I don't know why the project suddenly regained my father's attention. Maybe he had been sidetracked by lack of money. Perhaps he began again because Uncle Bob (Dad's younger brother) bought his family a sixteen-foot fiberglass boat with a 50hp outboard. For whatever reason, the wooden bones were fleshed out overnight. Launched when I was ten, Dad's boat had a white plywood hull and turquoise deck. Mom upholstered the front and rear bench seats in white Naugahyde tuck and roll. A 70hp Willy's jeep engine powered the craft christened *Ski-Daddle* by my Aunt Anne. It rode stable, high and fast in the water, the brass bell clanging.

Skis

While we drove around town with granddaughters in the back, my wife decided she'd find out what they really wanted for Christmas. The youngest had no interest in the conversation and used her default response of *stuffed animal.* The seven-year-old, however, was very specific. She wanted a cash register from Staples. My wife suggested it might be best to ask Santa for a gift that expensive, but our granddaughter was insistent. It had to come from Staples and not from Santa she explained. She wanted a real cash register, not one the elves made out of wood.

Life with my father was like being in the presence of

Santa's most talented elf. Although he never had a particularly festive disposition, there was nothing the man couldn't shape from wood. Looking back at his lifetime of projects, I finally appreciate those skills and realize what an elite craftsman he is. However, as a child there were more times when I wished we just bought real stuff like other people.

Diana was eight and Frank five by the time powerboats and water skiing became our extended family's main recreation. After building *Ski-Daddle* and forced to pay thirty-two dollars for a pair of varnished plywood skis, Dad accepted another challenge. He moved quickly from duplicating the store-bought doubles to crafting fine singles for slalom skiing, each custom fitted for our individual heights and weights. As he perfected the sophisticated jigs and laminating techniques, each ski was more elaborately beautiful.

He mostly worked with pine, birch, and mahogany, sometimes combining contrasting wood colors and textures as when he trimmed white pine skis with red mahogany. My father's art was always functional. From metal, he formed custom skegs for improved stability and maneuverability. He also devised an unobtrusive brass attachment that shot a rooster tail of water at even the slowest speed. Later he added wooden water sleds, trick disks, and shoe-size skis to his inventory.

In the beginning, we assumed Frank was too young to enjoy long weekends at the bay, but Brother Babe never grew bored. He skied all day with us. On doubles he'd cut sharply across the wake, drop one, and slalom through the buoys and perilous boat traffic. He learned to *snap off* from the beach, make the loop, coast to the shore and step right out of his ski cups onto the sand without getting wet. Eventually, Babe even tamed the skeg-less shoe skis. One day, he even skied barefooted!

Babe really did all these things when he was five years old; it's just his skiing was done on sand, twenty yards from the water's edge. Balancing on a beached ski and gripping padded handles of a yellow, nylon rope, Frank spent hours perfecting his style.

I don't remember who coaxed our six-year-old brother from sand to sea for the first time, but it was disastrous. Cruelly, he was dragged underwater for ten yards before releasing the rope. Shaken but not crushed, Babe cheerfully returned to his safer, better world of sand skiing. He didn't venture into the water again until he was nine. Then, after a few false starts, he mastered the skis in less than an hour.

Men, Babies, And Cars

My toddler brother was fascinated with the family automobile. One of his favorite trips was to the local Mobile

Oil filling station, Home of the Flying Red Horse. Imitating sound made by the station bell, Frank called it *going to the ging-ging.*

Youngsters today may not know gas stations used to be called service stations. In the 50s, when your car approached gas pumps, tires flattened a rubber hose that rang a large bell mounted over the office's front door. The clanging bell was the signal for a uniformed attendant to swarm your car. This man pumped gas, checked water and oil, washed windshields, aired tires if needed, and gave customers free plastic-handled steak knives with every fill up of ten gallons or more. Such frenzy so excited my little brother that he played gas station at home.

Everyone thought it was cute when he danced around Dad's car, kicking the tires or pretending to wash windows. He was not as adorable the day he filled the family car with gasoline. Dad discovered Frank crouched near the car's left, rear fender with a blue pail. As Babe meticulously shoveled gravel and white sand into the Chevy's uncapped tank, my little brother quietly sang to himself, "*Ging-ging. Ging-ging.*"

As much expense and aggravation as sand in the gas tank caused, at least it was a one time occurrence. Looking back, I marvel more at our father's long-suffering patience whenever he drove with us kids in the backseat; especially during the driving marathons we called family vacations. In those days, a successful vacation was one that covered the most miles in the least possible time. Sometimes we did so much nonstop driving our vacation photos all were taken from a window of the moving car. In fact, not until the film was printed were we entirely sure where we'd been or whether we had a good time. Past family vacations taught Diana and me, there was no chance we'd ever stop to see The Thing or stay overnight at one of those concrete tepee motels.

Disappointment had so worn us down that our silence could be bought with cheap coloring books and comics. The most we hoped for was occasional malt and fries at some truck stop during a midday pit stop. Our toddler brother, however, stayed engaged for hundreds of miles at a time. Without nagging seat belt laws, Babe rode standing behind Dad the entire way. He rested his crossed arms atop the driver's seat so his grinning face hovered over Dad's right shoulder. To an oncoming car, it probably looked like our driver had two heads. From the backseat, Frank looked like an oversized bobbin' head doll.

Impeded vision aside, I can't fathom how our father navigated to the incessant accompaniment of Frank's driving sounds. In congested areas with traffic lights every few blocks, Babe's chanted "Red means stop. Green mean go. Red means stop. Green mean go. Red means..." Even after the lights, quiet was temporary because of Babe's spirited imitations of revving engines and squealing tires. His sound effects were delivered at the same deafening level for even the slightest turn of the wheel and gentlest acceleration or braking.

Dad never pulled off the road and smacked Babe, but from the backseat I glimpsed how big the veins got in his neck. That might explain our father's penchant for traveling late at night across vast, straight stretches of Southwestern desert and why the phrase, "Aw, Honey, it's only another two hundred miles," was heard so often.

CHAPTER 11

Knowing Your Place

Safety First

During the first month of sixth grade, I was one of several lieutenants on the Safety Patrol. Next month I was promoted to captain and became second in command to our sponsor, Mr. Gabriel. When I graduated from elementary school, I retired as major which Mr. Gabriel commemorated with a framed certificate featuring my name and final rank handwritten in silver ink. The paper looked old and official like our classroom copy of the Declaration of Independence. But there was a lot of hard work before that day arrived.

As the faculty sponsor, Mr. Gabriel met regularly with his captain (me!) to complete duty rosters, plan training sessions, and create an inspection schedule. Each school day required three, three-man traffic patrols (one for the crosswalk at the school's office entrance and crosswalks on two roads adjacent to the school ground.) Additionally, those posts were manned three times a day (before school, during lunch, and dismissal). During lunch periods, patrolmen also were posted along the covered sidewalks to cut down on running and horseplay.

Naturally, the Safety Patrol was regularly excused from class early to change clothes and reach their assigned posts. Our uniform was white duck pants, a white dress shirt, black leather belt, and black dress shoes. Over those basics, we wore red knit cardigans and yellow military caps with red piping. Rank (again, military style) was displayed on patches sewn to our sweaters' upper sleeves and insignia pins on the caps. Mr. Gabriel called cadence as we practiced marching on the asphalt playground after school.

Marching was a necessary skill because each squad (one sergeant carrying a staff to control access to the crosswalk and two men using stop signs on long poles to halt traffic on either side of the crosswalk) traveled a considerable distance to their stations.

Our traffic signs were deployed with precise choreography, orchestrated by the sergeant's whistle blasts. While waiting to assist students, as cars whizzed by, the squad stood at parade rest. It was serious business. Monthly inspections took place on a patch of grass between two classroom pods. Mr. Gabriel wore one of his black suits during those ceremonies. He also wore white gloves, a red sash, and a silver sword with scabbard. He could have led us anywhere.

Oh, The Humanity

I was never a jock. As a kid I was pretty strong and had decent coordination. I was smart enough to learn rules and strategies so I was easy to coach. I always hustled but I wasn't a natural. Never the first one picked but never the last one either.

Some men risk multiple hernias playing in senior city leagues. Others abandon team sports for the relative safety of golf or jogging. The truly hopeless forego physical activity altogether and watch others play. Television enables an old jock (or never was) to scream at multi-million dollar professionals while he eats pork rinds and tells himself that he could have been #7 with the same breaks. The saddest men seek glory through their children.

Having said all that, I'm the first to admit it's unfair. Sports and fathers and sons were the rule during my childhood and probably always will be. My dad once built an elaborate basketball goal in our backyard and awed me with lay-ups and three-pointers. Basketball was his sport of choice when he was a youngster. Predictably, it wasn't mine. I was too chunky. I was okay at set shots but didn't move the ball well. It's natural a father wants to teach his boy what he knows best. It is also natural a son might feel a failure when his father's lessons don't take. If that was sometimes true of my childhood, then I accept the burden. I'll never believe he intended it to happen. Between a father and son there is much at stake and it's easy to misread hearts.

Baseball is the first organized sport I ever played and the only one I ever really loved. It made the most of my strengths and was most forgiving of my weaknesses. In Southern California during the late 1950s and early 60s, baseball was king and people took the game seriously. My first glove was a burgundy, clamshell-shaped thing with black plastic lacings. The pocket was silver printed with the signature of Gil Hodges. When I was 7, I didn't have a clue who that was, but it seemed pretty special and I was proud.

In those days, developing baseball prodigies was too important to leave to well-meaning parents. First, consider the number of young boys who came of baseball age each year in a metropolitan area like San Diego County. Consider, too, the damage done by allowing faulty batting stances and ball handling techniques to fester unchecked in unsupervised backyards and sandlots. The enormity of the problem made no solution too radical. Our parents, the generation who mobilized a sleeping America after Pearl Harbor, rallied to save American baseball from mediocrity. They approached the task using the same energy and strategies they'd used to smash the Axis powers. We were eight when my draft- aged schoolmates and I were summoned to our first baseball clinic. The school's intercom blared the date and time weeks in advance. I was nervous but ready.

Finally, one spring Saturday with parents in tow, hundreds of us gathered at the high school practice fields. It was an immense dirt area with three baseball diamonds side-by-side. Uniformed coaches with clipboards and silver whistles manned the dozen card tables in the adjacent parking lot. After forever, Mom and I stood before the table marked *E-F*.

"Got your money? Got your papers? Sign here, Kid. He'll get his uniform later, Ma'am." Then he added, "Pin this to your shirt, Kid. Group A, number 16." I couldn't believe I lost sleep for this. The Clinic was supposed to be a big deal but apparently anyone with a birth certificate, a signed permission slip, a doctor's form, and five bucks could belong to this man's army. Adult reality can be very ugly to an eight year old. It was about to get uglier.

Even a herd of cattle has a collective instinct for survival, but we of Group A never saw it coming. When told to, we moved obediently onto the dirt field and huddled around a white, painted stake. Incredibly, we weren't suspicious even when the coaches formed a concentric circle whose perimeter was about fifteen yards beyond our own. Experienced eyes would have understood what their demeanor foreshadowed. These weren't the same men who joked with such bravado in the parking lot. Now caps shaded silvered aviator sunglasses. Jaws were cruelly set. Pens and clipboards were poised in awful anticipation. Still, we never saw it coming.

To an outsider, I'm certain there was an innocent air to our jostling and excited chatter. Everything was to change momentarily. My last clear memory was one perimeter coach saying something like, "Well, men, it's time to separate the sheep from the goats." Glancing up and away from my friends, I glimpsed his clipboard raised high. Obviously, he was signaling, but to whom? Suddenly, to my far left, there were four, distinct, staccato cracks followed by faint whistling as something overhead cast birdlike shadows at my feet. Then came a thud followed by a bloody scream. Tommy was the first to go down.

None of us said anything. We just stared at Tommy's prone, writhing body and then at each other with uncomprehending eyes. Before we made sense of it, there was another thud, another scream. Then came more crying as each mortar struck its target with increasing rapidity and deadly effect. Panic replaced paralysis and someone finally shouted, "There. Over There! They're hittin' BALLS at us! Run for your life!" I turned to see four men - coaches - smacking balls at us from the edge of the parking lot. Teenaged boys held gunnysacks of baseballs and fed the frenzied batters as one might aid a machine gunner by guiding an ammo belt.

Behind the gunners, fathers stood with arms linked and their backs to the killing fields. Together they formed a flesh wall to cordon our sobbing mothers. Bloody-nosed boys stampeded and trampled the fallen as baseballs rained from the sky. I saw one tiny guy with blackened eyes break from the circle only to be tackled by a coach and returned to the melee. Oh the humanity. They say in combat a soldier develops a sixth sense about his mortality. I know this is true. That Saturday morning, when I was just eight years old, I heard the baseball with my name on it.

Frozen, I stared heavenward as the arcing baseball fell toward my face. As I vacantly considered my imminent demise, my short, pathetic life replayed itself before my eyes. Just then, an unfamiliar feeling awakened within my soft, spoiled, urban body - a kind of primitive, protective reflex. Involuntarily, my gloved hand rose above my head until the mitt blocked my vision of the speeding death ball. I closed my eyes. I probably prayed. SMACK! It was over.

I can't be certain how much time passed before I reopened my eyes. I only know there were no more colliding bodies, no more screams, and no more horror; just the muffled whimpers of fallen brothers. Somewhere in the distance a robin sang. My muddled prayer of gratitude was interrupted by one of the coaches. "Jack!" he yelled, "Number 16. We've got another fielder." Then he slapped me on the back. "Good job, Kid," he laughed. Only then did I realize my glove was still clenched over my head. I dropped my arm and opened my fist to inspect the mitt's pocket. There it was. My Gil Hodges had snagged that baseball of death and I was *alive!*

Extra Innings

And that is how my career in baseball began. As far as I know, nobody in Group *A* was killed that day. However, some were severely maimed. Some demanded their mamas and never returned. Others, after a little ice and a damp washcloth, would try again. A few of us, including me, made the first cut. We would be ballplayers.

That same day, I became an outfielder. When the fly ball massacre survivors were asked what position they wanted to learn, predictably almost everyone said pitcher or first baseman. I didn't see the odds in fighting 50 or 60 kids for a handful of spots. I just wanted to play so volunteering for the outfield improved my chances considerably.

In the coming weeks, we were divided into several clinic teams. Our mascot was a vulture. The most advanced players wore orange vulture shirts, the less advanced wore gold. When you made the orange team, Little League coaches scouted you. Fortunately, with time, most of us were invited to try out. At that level, coaches were given points to bid on players after watching weekend batting and fielding exhibitions. Little League assigned players to either major or minor league rosters. To be in the majors meant wearing a full baseball uniform (rather than just a t-shirt and cap) and playing on the best field. I made the majors as a Tiger.

These were golden days. I probably enjoyed practices as much as the games. At home I looked forward to Dad playing catch with me and giving advice about hitting and fielding. Looking back, I can't believe the sacrifice my folks made when they spent $27.95 for my first, all-leather Wilson glove. We bought it at Unimart, a membership discount store. (I think Uncle Bob got us in.) Mom and Dad whispered negotiations while I tried on the glove and tested the pocket. I never expected such a beautiful thing would ever be mine.

Although my brief professional career didn't even include Pony League, I have some glorious memories. During one game I stole two home runs from the same opposing batter by snagging balls at the fence line. I know the catches were mostly dumb luck and because my glove was huge, but it still felt great. As a batter I didn't hit homeruns (usually singles and doubles) but I slugged some serious RBI. I remember standing in left field on manicured grass, checking the batter's count on the electric scoreboard (donated by a local bank), and trying to envision my best throw if he should hit to me.

Maybe the real action wasn't in the outfield but I liked it there. When my team had the field, the coaches always wanted us to *look alive* and *chatter* to rattle the hitter. *He-ey, batta-batta.* I thought that was stupid and unnecessary. Out there I could mime the sounds and no one was the wiser.

I liked my big league uniform and the big league dreams it engendered. I enjoyed the ritual of shaping a new cap until the bill and crown were perfect. Even now I can smell the Neatsfoot oil we used to make our gloves soft and the pocket sweet. I feel the warmth of summer sun on my face and neck and the rush of coolness as an unexpected breeze hits my perspiring skin. I hear the click of my cleats on the dugout's concrete floor. I also feel the blousing rubbers that hold my socks cut into my fat calves. I remember how my stomach often was nervous before a game and how increasingly it didn't go away.

As the seasons continued and parents became more interested and too angry, I remember times when I prayed the kid in front of me would be the third out (and I wouldn't) and the game would be over even if it meant losing. But baseball didn't begin that way for me.

When it was just the guys and me, Mike was Mantle and I was Maris and we battled to break The Babe's record. No professional athlete would believe it, but on sandlots curve balls bend like rainbows, triple plays are the rule, and home run flies never fall back to earth.

Too Good To Be True?

When I was 8, building a collection of army men was my raison d'etre. At the time, my weekly income was 25¢. The toy store I shopped featured a bin of loose plastic soldiers for 5¢ each. That meant, after adding sales tax, I could buy only four soldiers a week even if I swore off movies, candy, and everything else of worth living for. My army wasn't growing fast enough and the hopelessness of my dilemma threw me into a pint-sized funk. At my lowest emotional ebb, hope burst forth in the form of a full-page, color advertisement in the back of my April edition of *Superman* comics. *200 WORLD WAR II SOLDIERS Only $1.98!* the headline screamed. *TWO ARMIES – THE AMERICANS, THE GERMANS!*

I may have been 8 years old, but I wasn't born yesterday. As badly as I wanted this to be true, I studied the text and accompanying illustration for loopholes. Certainly the drawing depicted a scene more elaborate than my sandbox tableaus - tanks, mortar blasts, and airplanes flying overhead - but, heck, my battlefields would look that good if I had 200 soldiers.

The ad's battleground featured hills thick with army men but, most importantly, every soldier's pose was identical to those of figures I already had accumulated. There was rifle-on-shoulder marching man, rifle-shooting guy (both standing and kneeling positions), prone sniper, machine-gun-on-tripod soldier, radioman, and minesweeping guy. If purchased separately at a store, such a collection would cost at least $10 plus tax. Worse, at my current income level, it would take 40 weeks to raise $10 plus tax. On the other hand, if I bought these soldiers through the mail, even after shelling out the required 25 cents for postage (no stamps please), I'd possess a magnificent army in about nine weeks. Why these Long Island and New York people so badly underestimated the value of army men was not my concern. If they were that stupid, they deserved to lose money.

I braced myself for nine weeks of scrimping to raise the purchase price, but my parents were so impressed by their child's unwavering dedication to a goal, after four weeks they exchanged my handful of coins for a check in the amount of $2.23. Mom even addressed the envelope. She also explained the concept of 4-6 weeks for delivery but that proved too abstract for my tunnel vision. Eventually I quit camping by the mailbox, convinced that any package big enough to hold an army of 200 plus tanks, jeeps, and airplanes would have to be delivered by truck, like Mom's lamps and end tables. I even theorized it would take two men to carry a box that big to our porch. As it happened, my soldiers arrived a month later with no great fanfare. They weren't shipped in a crate but in an 8″ X 10″ manila envelope nearly lost among the day's bills and advertising flyers.

My heart sunk when I recognized the envelope's return address. Then I grew furious because obviously those New York crooks hadn't sent everything in one shipment. There'd better be a letter of explanation inside, I thought, but the envelope contained only an invoice and my army. Rifle guy, machine gun guy, and a couple of others fell and bounced across the counter when I tapped the envelope empty. I was too sick to count, but there could have been 200 others between the folds of tissue paper I pulled from the mailer.

Later, my parents spent a lot of time explaining why I had no basis for a law suit. The crooks' advertisement hadn't lied so much as not tell the whole truth. Everything promised in the illustration was in the envelope. Indeed, there was an American army (green) and a German army (gray), plus several tanks, trucks, and jeeps (but no airplanes). What the crooks left unsaid was that their army men were identical to the large, flexible, beautifully detailed sculptures available from my local toy store in every way except size. Instead, their chintzy imitations were mere plastic slab silhouettes, less than an inch tall and no thicker than a box top.

I felt like the guy in that *Twilight Zone* episode who exchanged his soul to always look as young as he did at that moment. The guy thinks he's put one over on the Devil. If he stays young forever, he'll never die. Unless he dies, he'll never have to surrender his soul. Then the guy finds out that although he'll remain forever young on the *outside* like the Devil promised, *inside* he is growing older and sicker every minute. So, as my parents explained, those New York guys weren't complete crooks, they just lied like the Devil.

A healthy adult reconciles such childhood nightmares as character-building experiences. My disproportionate rage over current news stories about corrupt businessmen and fraud suggests I have some lingering issues.

Kool-Aid Kids

Being cash poor wasn't unusual and certainly not shameful for kids. In fact, having nothing but optimism fed our entrepreneurial instincts. Most kids tried the lemonade or Kool-Aid stand gambit at least once. The biggest problem running a drink stand was refusing thirsty friends without cash. Another practical complication was obtaining stock cheaply enough make a profit. Sold in nickel packs, powdered Kool-Aid mixed with two quarts of water. Flavor-Aid (Kool-Aid's less popular rival) was cheaper but not as good tasting. Besides, both brands required adding a cup of sugar, which was the biggest expense. Although moms did a lot of baking, it was hard to borrow that much white sugar undetected. Even when we made lemonade using real lemons, kids complained it needed sugar. Actually, most customers preferred lemonade made from cans of sweetened concentrate and that was really expensive.

A good way to distinguish your drink stand from competing sellers was to offer snacks in addition to drinks. Being kids ourselves, we knew what our customers enjoyed, but again the problem was startup capital. One solution, which often led to trouble, was scrounging supplies from home. I remember one particularly profitable day ended abruptly after we were caught selling cookies from Mom's Tupperware stash. (She baked for the entire month in weekend-long marathons and hid the containers of in the back of kitchen cabinets.)

Another time, when trees in our backyard bore exceptional crops of peaches and apricots, we added fruit to the menu without our parents' permission. Since the fruit-laden trees were stripped locust-bare only as high up as we could reach, it didn't require stellar detective work to tie us kids to the crime. Worse, we had harvested the peaches and apricots a month too early. For all the grief we earned ourselves, there wasn't a market for buckets of green fruit the size and hardness of golf balls.

Before being shut down by Mom a second time, one door-to-door popcorn sales venture promised to be the most lucrative of our lives. Pilfered lunch sacks from the pantry reduced our outlay, but the real coup was locating a nearly unlimited supply of popped corn. Literally, we had crates of free popcorn to fill free sacks for pure profit! Days earlier, Mom's two new living room lamps arrived by truck. The base of each lamp was a sculpted, ceramic swirl like a barber pole, about three feet tall, and topped with a drum-shaped fabric shade. To cushion the lamps during transit, both shipping crates were filled to the top with popped corn.

When my sister and I found the discarded packing near the back street trashcans, we couldn't believe our luck. Diana and I made four dollars before Mom found out. (A neighbor had phoned complaining about our stale-tasting popcorn.) Mom was really angry but also seemed worried, mumbling distractedly about chemicals and bugs. Although we offered to give the customers their money back and explain the situation, Mom nixed that plan. We agreed it would remain our special secret and not be mentioned again.

For all our spunk, my neighborhood never organized shows to raise money like the kids in *Our Gang* comedies, maybe because none of us had musical talent or a barn. Still, at least once each summer, whether born from need or simple boredom, someone decided a neighborhood carnival would make us rich. *Carnival* is too grand a word to describe the results. We confined activity to the small space of someone's front lawn. If moved to a backyard, we missed chance customers passing by.

We had no Ferris wheel or merry-go-round and nobody owned a pony, so we made substitutions. A decorated Radio Flyer hauled the smallest kids. Older customers paid to ride bikes whose frames were wrapped in colored crepe paper and decorated with handlebar streamers. Some bikes, using just a baseball card and clothespin, made motor sounds whenever the thick cardboard brushed the wheel's spinning wire spokes.

To keep things festive, workers wore remnants of last year's Halloween costumes. Music from an indoor turntable played loud enough to be heard through an open bedroom window. Simple snacks like saltines and jam were served and we sold unwanted, broken toys from our closets. Anyone owning an exotic pet, like a chameleon or soft-shell turtle, was encouraged to offer them for paid viewing. Without wooden milk bottles for a baseball throw, our patrons paid a nickel to knock stuffed animals from atop a picnic bench for penny candies. Many of the games on our midway, like Bingo and pin-the-tail-on-the-donkey, were familiar from neighborhood birthday parties.

Actually, the carnivals were compressed versions of our everyday lives. They failed as moneymakers because they offered nothing novel. Besides, since nearly everyone worked in the carnival, customers were scarce. It was like a pyramid scheme: success depended upon a continuous infusion of other people's money. Otherwise, we just redistributed the same pathetic handful of coins. Ultimately, none of this mattered because our carnivals always ended like Woodstock and became a free concert. When we quit worrying about money, we enjoyed ourselves. After we drank Kool-Aid and divided the last frosted graham crackers, we swapped broken toys before going home.

Knock, Knock

One time or another, most of my friends sold things like seeds, Grit magazine, greeting cards, or salve sent on approval by companies with addresses in Long Island or New Jersey.

Once or twice, I also succumbed to pipedreams of being a grade school mogul in my spare time. My early sales chops were honed during a short stint in the Cub Scouts. There I developed a door-to-door technique that was both direct and absolutely ineffective. Rather than prolong the haggling process I found excruciating, my opening pitch contained every reason they shouldn't buy from me. *"Nobody needs 50 sympathy cards and the glues on the envelopes don't stick, but..."*

My den mother quashed any future I had in sales. She had an indefensible habit of saddling us kids with impossible fundraiser products like gunny sacks of used light bulbs and three foot squares of bee's wax for candle making. When local sales bottomed, she forced us into her station wagon and used us like Travellers or gypsy scammers in faraway neighborhoods. Imagine being a chubby, shy eight-year-old standing on some stranger's doorstep in a cub uniform, forced to hawk five-pound tins of ground black pepper. *("You don't want any pepper do you?")* The truth is, failure to meet her impossible quotas got me drummed out of the Scouts before I earned even a Bear badge.

Despite the humiliation that accompanied every selling job I ever had, sales was the best option among childhood's limited avenues to serious money. No amount of emotional scarring could make me immune to comic book promises. The lure of cash plus prizes like English racing bicycles, camping equipment, fishing gear, and footballs was too seductive. Our comic books were filled with full-page ads that featured testimonials by smiling boys who looked just like my friends and me. The boys in the ads waved fistfuls of dollar bills. Saying *yes* to selling salve changed their lives, they insisted. The stuff practically sold itself, they swore. The pitch was irresistible but the promises never kept. At least not for me.

I'm sure someone, somewhere that summer in these contiguous United States won an English three-speeder with two-tone leather saddlebag, chrome generator-driven headlight and florescent handlebar streamers, but when the threatening letters came, I returned my unsold product immediately. Incredibly, the same company let me sell their flower seeds that winter (with no greater success). Experiences like those made my grandparents' coins, given with no strings but love, even more precious and remarkable. To honor their memories, I am the sucker for any child salesman who knocks on my door.

And Another Thing…

If materialism is uglier today, it isn't because people are less moral than in the good old days. Achieving balance in life has never been easy, but the world's lopsided distribution of wealth makes Americans particularly vulnerable. The deluge of redundant goods drowning us is possible because of cheap foreign labor. When Americans quit being builders, our work became consuming and gluttony a measure of achievement and patriotism. Temptation is compounded when there's more stuff to buy, more pressure to buy it, and enough credit to allow anyone to indulge, at least for a while. There is nothing inherently wrong with material things but problems arise when *fashion* is confused with *quality* and *want* cannot be sorted from *need*. When we finally get our fill, we'll have to search elsewhere for sustenance. Perhaps excess can make us a nation of Gandhis.

I Disagree, Mr. Berger

Both sisters are good girls but the younger granddaughter has a streak of lawyer. The older is typically an adult pleaser and rule-obsessed. Her biggest aggravation is running herd on her sibling when they travel without Mom and Dad. Involved parents that they are, the girls don't visit without being read their Miranda Rights: don't ask your grandparents for money or gifts, do as they say, eat what they serve, clean up your messes, and go to bed early or you'll have hell to pay when you get home. Both girls are of elfin stature so they've always traveled buckled on boosters in the car's back seat. That arrangement has made my wife and me privy to amazing conversations.

From the first time the younger spoke, their differences were obvious. One telling exchange occurred when they were pre-school and second grader. We weren't 5 minutes into the half hour drive to our apartment when the younger began listing her wants, "You know what you could buy me, Grandma?"

Predictably, Jiminy Cricket tried to shame little sister with the reminder, "Momma said not to ask for stuff."

The younger's retort was immediate. "Well, Momma's not here, is she?"

It was the kind of disregard for protocol that drives the older to tears of frustration. My wife and I made a show of smoothing over their squabble but privately expressed admiration for the little one's ability to ferret out truth so quickly.

Of course we intended to let them have or do anything they wanted during the next 24 hours, regardless of what Momma said. For big sister's sake, we tried to make her wishes sound like our ideas.

Money, Money

No one spoils a child with less concern about retarding character development than a grandparent. In the old days, kids were paid allowances for completing weekly chores. Actually, parents had a pretty sweet deal. They got cheap domestic labor as their children learned the value of work and rudiments of capitalism. Without collective bargaining, we had to accept all assignments and an arbitrary wage scale based more on parental whim than merit. By their rules, I wouldn't earn 50¢ a week until I was 10, no matter how hard I worked. However, whenever the grandparents visited, it was a whole new ball game.

Heck, if grandparents didn't arrive with a gift in hand, they wanted to take you to a toy store immediately. Sometimes Grandma gave me a quarter just for watching TV with her, something I would have done for free. Although the cash came with no conditions, her expectations didn't always reflect my reality – "You should go to the movies, Honey. Get popcorn and soda, maybe an ice cream on the way home. And don't you even worry about bringing me change." (I think the average yearly income when she was young must have been about $50.)

Still, a quarter was a goodly sum during my free-range years. Expressed another way, 25¢ was five plastic army men, a paper kite (but no string), five packs of baseball cards (five cards each and a slab of pink gum), two comic books and change (or one fat annual edition), a quart of Bubble-Up, a sack of penny candy, the middle-sized balsa glider (the one without rubber band driven prop and wheels), a bag of metal jacks and ball for your sister, a gallon of gasoline for your father's car, or one *admission* to the movies.

Twenty-five was a mystical number during my childhood, not dissimilar to the Bible's *3, 40,* or *1000.* My world was configured from multiples of 5.

For example, even the neighborhood variety store where I did my personal shopping was called *5¢, 10¢ & 25¢ Up.* Nickel, dime & quarter. My first weekly allowance was 25¢. Subsequent raises made it 50¢, 75¢, and finally a dollar. In the 1950s a quarter a week purchased a child's basic needs, but quality and novelty cost more. If a boy was satisfied with a drawstring sack of cat eyes (no puries, rainbows, boulders, peewees or steelies) or a *wooden* yo-yo (plastic Duncan Imperials began at $1.25), there was no problem. But whenever a guy desired anything pricier than a gyroscope, options dwindled quickly.

Adult solutions centered on patience and saving. That's a hard sell when a kid is under the spell of something as grand as a three-stage water rocket (w/satellite) guaranteed to reach an apogee of 500 feet, for instance. With my income, saving $4.75 required an absurd amount of patience.

As a parent myself, rather than crush their dreams outright, I ask my children to visualize their material desire (like a swell water rocket, for instance) as being made from quarters rather than plastic. I then suggest those quarters aren't merely coins; rather each represents a week of chores and sacrifice. The true price of consumerism is exposed when framed for children in such a strikingly visual manner. Most foolish purchases can be avoided if they are first deferred. Unfortunately, visualization exercises never kept me from buying X-Ray Spex or that water rocket whose second stage and satellite got lost the first time I launched it.

Free-range parents were contractually obligated to buy toys only on birthdays and Christmas (possibly Easter). That was the agreement everyone lived by. However, even those occasions weren't always the slam-dunks they should have been because shopping for a child without the child's supervision is always an opportunity for disaster. (Think how many *Beetle* albums well-intentioned adults purchased.) Even when supplied with visual aids like bookmarked toy catalogs and circled newspaper ads, mistakes were common because few adults have a child's eye for detail. Anyone who has devoted two months of intense study to a Sears Christmas catalog knows not all boats and talking dolls are alike.

Still, even the wrong toy usually was preferable to a gift of cash. Sometimes a well-meaning, distant relative sent money so the child could choose his or her own gift, but parents routinely routed cash gifts into one of those notorious college savings accounts, which when you're 10 is the same as no present at all. In fact, the more generous the cash gift, the less likely the child would even hold the money. We were devious but never sophisticated enough to launder birthday checks.

Obstacles like these encouraged creative cash raising strategies. Visiting dinner guests provided several funding opportunities. Some scams, like chatting -up adults, required a child young enough to pull off *cute* while wearing those one-piece pajamas with feet and door in the back. The routine involved carrying a coin bank into the living room and asking company to *feed the pig*. At the very least, loose change could be harvested from beneath the sofa and chair cushions when company left. Empty bottles were another opportunity provided by adult guests.

Back then, soda wasn't an everyday drink. Rather, it was reserved for entertaining and special occasions. Adults might have hogged the drinks, but kids got the empties to cash for deposits. Each recyclable bottle in an RC Cola six-pack, for instance, brought 3 cents and an additional 5 cents for the cardboard carrier. Different brands and different sized bottles brought varying amounts, but the cash added up pretty fast. Piggly Wiggly clerks always pressured us kids to apply bottle deposits toward more soda from their store. However, if we did our business quickly, the counter guy at the liquor store cashed bottles with no questions or comments. It was easy money. Sometimes we bought beef jerky from a big jar next to his register.

Nobody could live lavishly on bottle deposits so we learned to stretch the cash we had. Pooling resources and splitting custody of purchased comics and issues of *Famous Monsters* was common. Sharing consumable goods was even more widespread and less complicated. By throwing in together, kids could buy bigger bags of chips or larger bottles of pop. Whenever possible, we chose lesser-known brands like Bubble-Up (*A Kiss of Lemon – A Kiss of Lime*) over national brands like 7-Up. Bubble-Up tasted a lot like 7-Up and cost the same, but came in 12-ounce bottles instead of 8. Need and greed made savvy shoppers but sometimes our bargain-hunting ways came back to bite us. How many free-range kids grew up to become Bernie Madoff victims?

CHAPTER 12

Heart's Desire

All Hallowed - Evens

Before being ruined by stories of molesters and candy tainters, Halloween was second only to Christmas as every kid's favorite pagan holiday. From twilight until midnight, costumed hoards invaded in waves. They roamed our neighborhood knocking on doors, determined not to leave until the last piece of candy was extracted. Our housing division was populated mostly by young, growing families who played along, so a kid could fill a paper shopping bag with candy in a couple of hours. Free and plenty, Halloween treats were a kid's manna.

Now I appreciate how ingenious were the Halloween costumes Mom made us. With a small thrift store purchase, a rubber nose, and 50 cents of grease paint, she once turned me into Freddie the Freeloader, complete with top hat and calico bundle on a stick. Her costumes for Diana and Frank were equally elaborate, but at the time we resented anything homemade. In contrast, our grandchildren prefer homemade. Recently, two granddaughters begged my wife to sew poodle skirts for their costumes. They were such a hit, the skirts were worn out from overuse before Halloween arrived.

We, on the other hand, wished for just once our parents would buy the things we needed. We dreamed of owning those swell dime store costumes, the ones with a plastic mask and silk pajamas that tied in the back. One Halloween, Mom gave in. The ill-fitting pajamas were itchy and masks so hot we couldn't wear them after 30 minutes and spent the rest of the evening explaining what our costume was supposed to be.

Nonetheless, no costume snafu ever kept us from our Halloween rounds. Beginning at the first house, Sister Diana and I devoured each piece of candy the moment it hit the bottom of our bag. When we stumbled home several hours later, both of us dragged sacks of empty wrappers and were descending rapidly into sugar comas. In contrast, little brother Frank's bag overflowed with untouched sweets.

At home, he nibbled a few candy corns while meticulously separating his treasure into several, equal assortments. He bundled the candy piles in wax paper secured with rubber bands. After taking inventory, Frank stashed the packages into the top box springs of our bunk bed through a small rip in the underside's cotton covering. Unlike Diana and me, Frank rationed his sugary windfall until Christmas when it would be naturally replenished. Even worse, he made Christmas candy last until Easter. Now, I'm not saying our brother was selfish. Sometimes, if we asked *real nice* or did favors for him, he'd share some of his precious candy with us in November but he'd be really snotty about it. I hope Frank savored his puny victories because they were few and far between.

Wishes

I was browsing the Target toy aisle, anticipating future needs of our infant granddaughter. My wife questioned whether my choices were based on the baby's interests or mine. Admittedly, I've been guilty of that, beginning with a wall clock I bought my toddler son. The clock was shaped like a black cat with bulbous eyes that moved back and forth in synchronization with the cat's pendulum tail. I would've cherished that clock at his age, but apparently sleeping in the same room with it proved so terrifying, my kid almost was driven into therapy. I still believe he over-reacted but, come to think of it, my father did stuff like that, too.

More than birthdays, Christmas was a kid's best shot at acquiring pleading-and-scheming-worthy toys. In my family, we could count on replenishing our socks and underwear drawers, and getting several smaller gifts like a baseball or some dominoes, but Santa also cut special deals with us. If we limited our wish list to a single big gift, he'd do his very best to deliver. That was a lot of pressure. Christmas catalogs from J.C. Penny, Sears, and Montgomery Ward arrived in October or early November. For the next several weeks, those catalogs were read more thoroughly than textbooks or family bibles. Frankly, more depended upon it.

I remember paging through the toy sections, showing Dad my latest candidates for The List. At that young age, I didn't know how Santa stayed current on Christmas wishes, unless he was like Jesus who was everywhere and heard everything. There was no proof my parents were anywhere in the Christmas chain of command, but I kept them in the loop.

Usually my top choice was a toy set like *Fort Apache* with dozens of plastic parts: gate and fence sections, log cabins, molded horses, armed cavalrymen, and marauding Indians. Rearranging the pieces in endless variation gave me pleasure. I liked miniature worlds so much that I drew windows, framed pictures, silhouetted furniture, and rugs on the inside walls of my bureau drawers. My inspiration was the interior of Jerry's mouse hole home in cartoons - matchbox bed, thimble lampshades, tables made from spools. Whenever I needed a playhouse for my toy figures, I just emptied my socks and underwear on the bedroom floor.

Dad patiently listened while I debated aloud the merits of *Fort Apache* vs. a *Marx Farm Barn,* but kept steering me back to the catalog's science section. The Sears catalog had two pages of model steam engines but the differences among them were too subtle for me. They all had the same water tanks atop simulated brick stands, large brass flywheels and pistons, working steam whistles, and were powered by mentholated spirits. I appreciated their detail but never understood how I'd play with one. Dad really wanted a steam engine that Christmas, but we asked for a Ben-Hur play set instead and Santa kept his promise.

Ben-Hur was an amazing toy set that included a coliseum, chariots, Roman soldiers and heathen citizens, even some Christians to feed to the lions. That year, Santa also included an expensive gift I didn't request -- *Mr. Machine.* Mr. Machine was a large wind-up robot on wheels that could be taken apart and reassembled. Its side plates were clear plastic, which made the interior gear works visible. However, Mr. Machine, engineering wonder that he was, didn't survive Christmas morning. While I was racing chariots, Dad pulled a pin from the robot's side. The instruction sheet he didn't read warned my father against disassembling the toy before its spring motor completely wound down. After the explosion, we never recovered enough gears to put Mr. Machine back together again. From that day, we kept his remains in a shoebox.

The Fox

One of the best things about Christmas Day was showing off new toys and seeing what everyone else got. Maybe because we wished from the same catalogs, Santa often delivered duplicate toys to our neighborhood. That could be a great thing, like the year everyone got ping-pong ball bazookas. Other times, it was a letdown, like the Christmas I got my Zorro outfit. I was so excited about the costume that I immediately put it on and slipped outside.

Wearing the black plastic, flat-rimmed hat; black plastic mask; black plastic cummerbund; and black rayon cape, I could have been Guy Williams' chubby stand-in if Zorro's standard getup also included striped pajamas. The sword was the coolest thing. Naturally, it too was made of plastic and couldn't cut anything, but a piece of chalk on the blade's tip made it possible to leave a signature Z anywhere.

The sun wasn't up and the lawn still damp with dew, but I was determined to greet my friends in character. Houses to the right of me, houses to the left of me, houses in front of me; I waited for the gang to emerge clutching Christmas toys, satisfied with their inferior gifts until they saw me. When first light peeked over the Whitmore's roof, I heard jostling front door locks and hardware all around. The neighborhood was awake.

With head thrown back and cape fluttering, I sliced the air thrice in morning salute. For greatest effect, I held that pose a very long time. Sadly, when I lowered my rapier, I beheld a terrible sight: Zorros to my right, Zorros to my left, Zorros in front of me. That Christmas morning, 8 Zorros competed to drive evil from the neighborhood. By noon, we fought each other to claim the last virgin fence section with a chalk Z.

EPILOGUE

All Good Things

A Mom And A Dad

If English were dead like Latin, it would be perfect. Living languages have exceptions to the rules that make them messy but vital. The stability of ideologies is similar: once a rigid belief system is exposed to life's untidiness, it's impossible to keep it pure. Stem cell research is immoral until your husband contracts Alzheimer's. Gays are an abomination unless your child is a lesbian. Divorces result from a lack of character until you are divorced.

My childhood home had two parents, something my own son can't remember. If it had been possible to choose, I'd have given him that same kind of home with brothers and sisters, too. Still, even with our early breakup, I was more involved in my child's everyday life than Dad was with me. This is an observation and not a reproach. I'm certain my father was more attentive than his father. This fact may be one of the few proofs that men, to some extent, are evolving.

Today, many families emphasize partnerships with more equitable divisions of labor. Responsibilities are not automatically determined by gender. My father's presence was conspicuous but home was more a refuge than his focus. When Dad came home we weren't passed from Mom's care to his, like a baton between relay runners. Rather, his usual role was to make money, head the dinner table, sign contracts, drive whenever the family traveled together, repair broken things, and serve as final arbitrator in any dispute not settled before he came home. Ultimately, decisions that affected us all were his, but Dad wasn't involved with dozens of lesser, daily decisions Mom made. Memories of him are often vignettes like surf fishing with my first green glass rod or hitting a baseball he pitched or him telling me, in an almost formal tone, how proud he was of my grades.

Recollections of Mom are less concise but certainly as enduring. Since she was the center of every waking hour, she is omnipresent in my earliest memories. Remembering her is more likely to conjure emotions than events. Even now, saying her name can summon security and warm waves of approval or stern admonishments to do what's right. The very shape of remembrances says more about the way the world used to be than about my family in particular. I can't imagine being raised in a single parent household like my son. During my childhood, it took two. Fathers commonly worked away from the homes where mothers raised children. I doubt my parents or their friends ever questioned this arrangement and, frankly, maybe they shouldn't have. From my perspective, it seemed to work very well for a very long time. I was oblivious to a hidden unhappiness that eventually wedged my parents apart, but that was years after I left home.

My thinking has always been emotional and muddled with inconsistencies. Despite some classic elitist tendencies, I am a Joe the Philosopher kind of guy. In a world comfortable with situational grays, I need absolutes – just not as many as some people do and not as absolutely. I'm pretty content to start and stop with The Ten Commandments or similar short lists found in most religious texts. After that, it's all legislating from the bench. Anyone aching to be America's moral gatekeeper only gets a place in a very long line. Not even a high school diploma and a radio show guarantees a prophet is fit to judge or lead.

I was raised with consistent, conservative values, but my presumptions about family (and other topics) didn't survive intact after exposure to the larger world. Working as a public school teacher provided real opportunity to see how others lived. Mostly I met traditional families, but also encountered single parent families navigating life with similar degrees of success and failure. The day a beaming student introduced his two moms proved no more disquieting than rationalizations of a pious couple who emotionally abused their child in the name of *tough love.*

When some boomers get nostalgic, they describe families I recognize only from old Disney movies. Their depictions imply America had a monopoly on morality when everyone lived the TV ideals of *Father Knows Best*. Certainly, my family was among many who tried, but even in the good old days there were single parent homes by choice, death, divorce, or abandonment. Even so, I'd bet many children from those damaged households also carry fond family memories. The mere presence of a mother and a father has never guaranteed children are nurtured with security and attention. It still doesn't.

Some define an ideal family as beginning with a man and woman who marry for love (before they have children). Anything short of a purposeful, life-long union that adds carefree, economically independent, patriotic children to the public tax roll is failure. (I'm a big fan of fidelity, but suggest adding a stipulation that spouses die within 24 hours of each other. This would provide closure for survivors and facilitate distribution of the estate.) For me, most descriptions of family are too limiting. People are welcome to live by strict tenets but that doesn't make them arbitrators of God.

Unless one resides in the 17th century, bloodlines aren't the ultimate measure of family. Is it even human to ration love according to something as arbitrary as position on a family tree? My sons and daughters are my children no matter what their surname, and their children are my grandchildren. Attaching the *step-* prefix simplifies introductions but misrepresents my love for them.

Family bonds are tested by death and divorce, but it is indecent to discard innocents when legal relationships change. Families of all configurations are maintained by acts of mutual compassion, not by invoking property rights and ancient codes of filial loyalty. Anyone wanting a family that requires no tears should live far, far away from anyone called kin. Safer yet, only devote energy to dead relatives because the living will always disappoint.

The most durable families are not composed of perfect individuals but people who love and forgive as perfectly as they are able. Kinship doesn't preclude bruised spirits (in fact, it guarantees conflict), but being family also presumes an irrevocable privilege of belonging. In a healthy kinship, after tempers cool, there's always a way back into the circle. Over the last sixty years, my family has committed sins against me that still chaff. Unintentionally, I've also inflicted the same pains (multiple times) on my own spouse, in-laws, and children. Failing others as I've been failed isn't an excuse, but it suggests not every hurtful thing is done deliberately. It also suggests limits to human perfectibility, whatever our good intentions.

My wife insists a long life doesn't change anyone for the better; we only become more like ourselves, she says. If Aunt Louise is obnoxious at 40, at 80 she will be obnoxiousness squared. If Cousin Roy is a hypochondriac, what except death will change him? To expect otherwise is as sensible as complaining about summer heat. As my lovely sage is fond of asking, "What part of *Texas July* do you not understand?"

Whenever I catch myself in a mirror or apologize to a teenage cashier because I've forgotten my cell phone number again, time travel sounds ever enticing. During sober moments, I know the cost of going backward is too dear, even in exchange for a subtle mind, thicker hair, and fewer chins. Re-inhabiting my youth would be like forcing a decorated soldier to endure basic training again. Surely the past merits reverence, mourning, and celebration but the past is not a destination. The greatest loves of my life are here and now.

My mother and father would deny anything extraordinary in their parenting but they are wrong. Because their marriage didn't last, they discount the importance of their time together and sometimes express guilt. The family of my free-range childhood is gone but another takes its place. Our family's worth never was tied to an era or television ideal. Even when grievous mistakes were made, love was evident. That was always enough for us kids then. It still is.

Cool Hand

Robert Ackerman was the coolest kid in the sixth grade. He was extraordinary the way the runt of a litter is or a cat with curious markings. He had a lopsided smile and heavy-lidded eyes like the actor Robert Mitchum except our Robert wasn't wild or dangerous. Plus his brown head was covered with short, tight curls. Although not particularly clever or accomplished, he was always chosen early for any team or classroom competition. Every girl fawned over him, yet guys rarely were jealous. Everybody smoothed the way for damaged Robert, even his teachers.

He learned to sleep while sitting erect with eyes wide open. That ability produced several entertaining exchanges when our teacher thought she was questioning someone attentive or at least conscious. Robert was the classmate most likely to dye himself blue by chewing through a soft plastic ink cartridge as he read. Whenever rotting smells permeated our classroom, the teacher's investigation began with Robert's desk. Still, I don't remember anyone holding grudges over his antics. That would be as senseless as beating a puppy.

I admired Robert Ackerman's penmanship. Left-handed, he wrote his cursive lessons with a backward slant. And though she tried to teach him properly, that was another battle the teacher lost. Robert certainly didn't write his way to be cool but it was. At home, with no one over my shoulder, I perfected a scrawling signature that combined John Hancock's flourishes and Robert's backhand. Actually, it felt pretty natural but I never turned in assignments with my name written like that. Sixth grade was the end of elementary school and my life in Southern California.

Most classmates would attend the same junior high the following school year but the Navy sent Robert's family to Hawaii and we moved to Arizona. My new bedroom wasn't unpacked when Tina wrote saying Robert Ackerman had died from a brain tumor. Her mother told her it was true. Before that moment, I'd never known anyone who died, short of distant relatives I supposedly met as a baby but didn't remember. This moment had no precedent. I felt damaged because I didn't know how to react. From that day I carried Robert's school photo in my wallet, one he signed *your friend*. My Arizona teachers never commented on my backhanded penmanship. Apparently, they fought bigger battles in junior high.

Making friends in a town populated by ranchers and cowboys was hard. Even though I was fat and not athletic, they called me a surfer because I had blond hair and came from California. Carpentry jobs proved scarce for Dad and then one of his retinas detached and we worried he might go blind. Our moving money from the California house sale ran out. My mother drove 30 miles round trip to clean motel rooms and I took a paper route although no one ever insisted I give my money to the family.

I had 28 daily customers on my country route and a few more Sunday only. To reach the paper drop each morning, I biked across a one lane bridge trafficked by speeding cement trucks from the local plant. Fortunately, in the dark I could gauge safe crossings by their headlights. On the other side, there was a closed café with a lit porch where I packed my newspapers. One October morning I got caught in the rain while crossing the bridge. I was soaked when I reached the café. I was worried about how I'd make my deliveries so the headline didn't immediately get my attention. *Soviet Missiles Found in Cuba* it read.

Beginnings

My neighborhood was like thousands of others that materialized after The War. That was when grass fields metamorphosed into tracts of neat, three-bedrooms for $5,000 and twenty-year mortgages. Trees were small and staked and front yards were tilled, ready for the first Bermuda seed. Uncracked sidewalks led to gleaming neighborhood schools that flew untattered forty-eight star flags. Clerks appreciated your business and stores were located within walking distance for your shopping convenience. My neighborhood had no history and that was its strength. My young parents were suburban pioneers - first houses, first children, first marriages.

Community pride felt genuine. Entertainments weren't as solitary then. There weren't barn raisings but we had barbeques and bowling leagues. That's not to say I can't remember adult gossip about men who drank too much or husbands and wives who fought. Occasionally, the competitiveness and pettiness was blatant, even to a child.

In free-range days it wasn't necessary to love your neighbor but, at the very least, you knew his name. Accordingly, men watched boxing on Wednesday night at our house because Dad's TV had the biggest screen. Mom gathered monthly with other women to drink tea, smoke, and eat pastel-colored butter mints while marveling at the latest Tupperware technology. During get-togethers, husbands and wives normally segregated themselves after banishing children to a bedroom or backyard. Mothers didn't appreciate kids overhearing their conversations but I liked listening to the men anyway because they talked about bigger things. My father's friends usually agreed on how to run the government and the world, but I remember grousing about Castro taking Cuba and confusion when Eisenhower admitted the U-2 was a spy plane, just as Khrushchev said.

Consumerism was not yet ugly. During my neighborhood's earliest years, no one had much, certainly no more than anyone else. It wasn't shameful to make family clothes or furnish a home one piece at a time and owning a washer and dryer qualified any housewife as Queen for a Day. Men with no reasonable hope of owning a Cadillac still were mesmerized when Detroit unveiled the latest fin and bullet taillight variation. Jealousy wasn't always the first reaction to someone else's latest purchase because the neighbor's success was a harbinger your own good fortune was just around the bend.

The only extraordinary thing about my family's life in Southern California is how conventional it was. It's tempting to make heroes of everyone we've loved and villains of those who've hurt us, though experience suggests often they're the same person. It is equally dishonest to attribute indiscriminately clearer vision and selfless courage to everyone who came before. Applying such a skewed measure makes it impossible to forgive anyone, including our self.

This is context for my free-range years, painted with the broadest brush. We lived in the eye of a storm, ignorant of the turbulence gathering speed around us. My family was imperfect in so many ways, but even now, I feel inexplicably safe when I remember us together.

ABOUT THE AUTHOR

The author (seen captured above) has lived in California, Arizona, and Oklahoma. Currently, home is Fort Worth, Texas, where he and his wife, Sue, became urban enthusiasts 6 years ago. Both write and teach. Current travel plans are dictated by completion of their state refrigerator magnet collection. Long-term plans include more international travel (regardless of refrigerator magnet availability). In addition to writing projects, he indulges a longtime interest in photography. Both John and Sue are pursuing black belts in grandparenting.

www.ingramcontent.com/pod-product-compliance
Lightning Source LLC
Chambersburg PA
CBHW020415180626
46812CB00003B/983

* 9 7 8 0 6 1 5 4 5 6 0 6 5 *